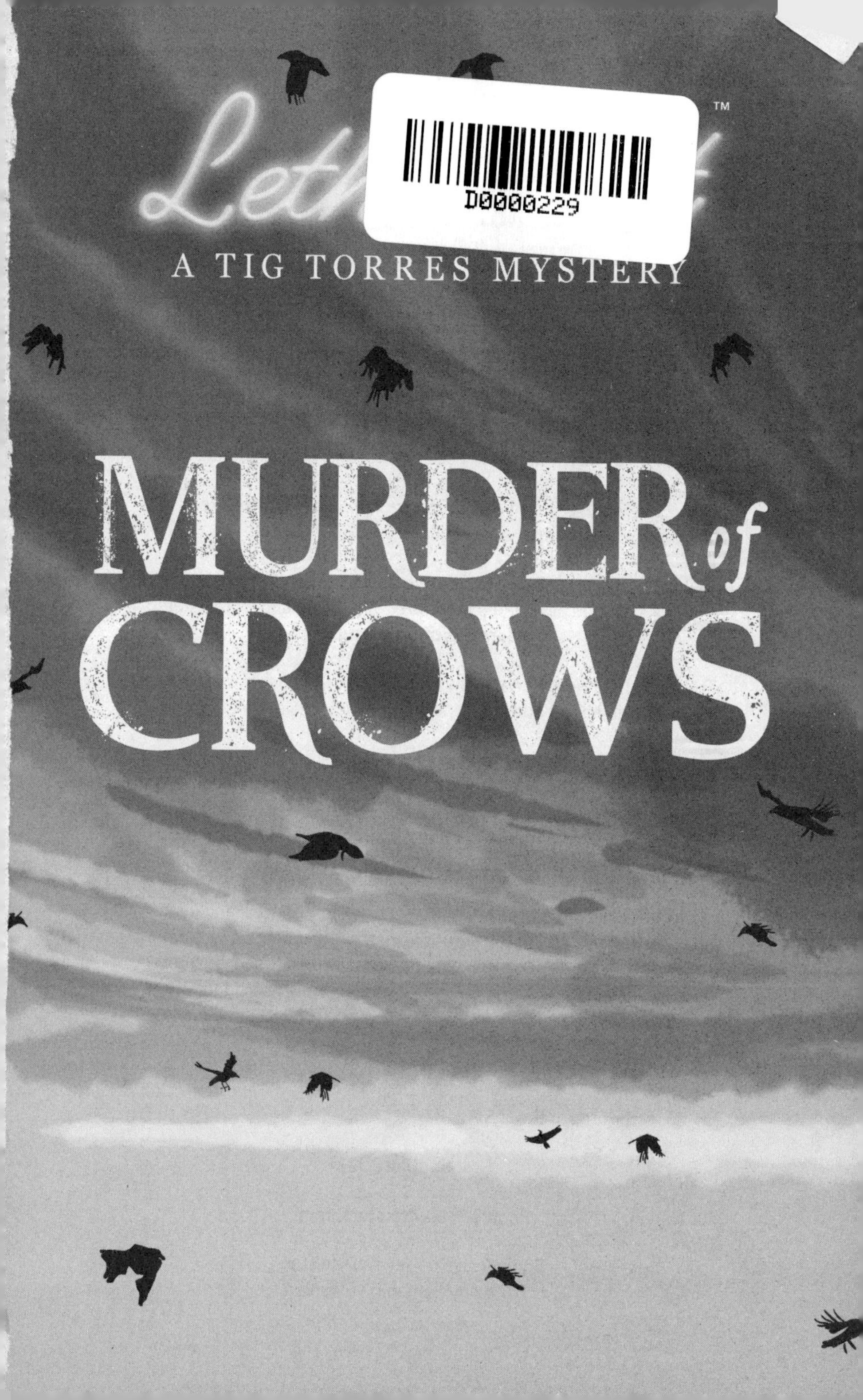
A TIG TORRES MYSTERY
MURDER of
CROWS

Lethal Lit

created by Heather Einhorn, Adam Staffaroni,
Alex Segura, and Monica Gallagher

EEP

ISBN 978-1-338-74292-3

1 2021

Printed in the U.S.A. 23

First printing 2022

Photos © Shutterstock.com

Book design by Jessica Meltzer
Edited by Samantha Swank

I would like to dedicate this to kids who see a thread and pull it. Who know that some trouble is good trouble and that they're always strongest with their friends by their side. –K. A.

Lethal Lit™

A TIG TORRES MYSTERY

MURDER of CROWS

An original novel by K. Ancrum

Scholastic Inc.

It was the summer of 1972.

Local librarian Jet Cassidy hurried across the street and up the church steps under the cover of darkness. It was nearly two o'clock in the morning, and the streets had long since cleared of potential witnesses. Tucked under his coat, he had gloves, a flashlight, a pistol, and a small piece of paper that was going to change his entire life.

The church doors were always open to the public, no matter the visitors' intentions. Jet slipped inside and strode quickly across the room. The girls he had overheard in the library had been specific. Tucked in the corner, where they thought no one was listening, they said the secret that would grant its seeker untold riches would be located somewhere up high, and there was nothing higher and older than the chandelier.

Taking a moment to listen to make sure the church was truly empty, Jet went up past the altar—farther than he'd ever gone as a member of the congregation. He followed a short hallway to the stairs that led to the double balconies: one for more congregation seating space for funerals and weddings, and the last a prayer sanctuary frequented only by the pastor himself.

The third floor was a small space, the slanted roof tilting in so sharply he was almost too tall to stand. Across from him at face height was the chandelier. Jet had never seen the fixture this close before. It was dark this high up. The wide stained-glass windows on the first floor provided very little moonlight to see by. Jet took out his flashlight and shined it at the chandelier, his eyes picking over the intricate brass fixture one filigree at a time.

There! Near the center, wrapped around the stem of a decorative leaf, was a small, tightly curled piece of paper tied to the twig with wire. The paper seemed to be wrapped around something—something shiny . . .

Jet looked down at the pews forty feet below him, then back at the chandelier hanging eight feet away from the edge of the balcony. Leaning against the wall was the candle snuffer the church staff used to put out the candles. All he needed was to pull the light fixture closer to the balcony edge and the treasure would be his . . .

The next morning, the steward opened the church doors to find Jet Cassidy's broken body smashed across the tops of the pews. His blood was sprayed across three floors in a pinwheeling arc that dashed the balconies, entrance, and altar in biohazard. The chandelier was shattered on the ground around him, the candle snuffer still hooked on its base after Jet's fatal grab. It took them three days to scrub the gore from the stone.

What no one realized was that the secret that had cost Jet Cassidy his life was already gone. Mere minutes after the librarian had fallen to his death, the clever girls he had tried to steal from crept into the church. Together, they had managed to pluck the paper—and the object wrapped inside—from the chandelier, exiting again with no one the wiser.

This time on Lethal Lit, join me, Tig Torres, on a mission to uncover the truth about a great and terrible mystery. A story of greed that began at the dawn of Hollow Falls's birth, stretching nearly two hundred years through time. All mentions of it burned out of our books, all witnesses sworn to silence—the mystery of a great treasure permanently hidden in plain sight. A treasure that some of our most respected townspeople would kill to find, and that others have killed to keep hidden.

It all revolves around a mysterious club with mysterious members: the Murder of Crows. Mr. Levinson, our beloved newspaper adviser turned violent serial killer, used this club as his hunting grounds—twisting his love of literature into a gory massacre that claimed many of its members.

I never thought my shadow would darken their door again. But if I've learned anything from all I went through after facing down the Lit Killer, it's that you can't bury your past, no matter how dark it is. The truth will always come to light—whether you want it to or not.

Abuela didn't believe that. She thought her history with The Hunt and the Murder of Crows could be forgotten. That it was just another mystery buried deep beneath the ground of Hollow Falls. But she was wrong. And look what happened.

I never thought I'd be back here, documenting another gruesome mystery for my loyal listeners in Hollow Falls. But I knew I had to find the founder's treasure before anyone else got killed. Before anyone else I loved got hurt.

No, you can't bury the past—so I guess I'm going to dig it up.

Chapter 1

It doesn't matter where you are on earth, one thing will always be true: Buses never come on time. I'd been sitting at the bus stop for over twenty minutes—way past the time the next bus should have come—and there was still no sign of it.

While no one could ever consider me, Tig Torres, a stickler for punctuality, there is a definite limit to everyone's patience, and I was rapidly reaching mine. School was a fifteen-minute bus ride away, but it had been a whole month and a half since I'd seen Wyn and Max. Max had mostly stayed in to recover from his attack by the Lit Killer, and Wyn's parents had dragged her off for summer vacation. Meanwhile, I had spent some time back in New York, trying to shake off the events of the previous spring. But even summer in the city couldn't make me forget what had happened.

Max, Wyn, and I had been texting and messaging one another, but we had yet to meet up in person. I couldn't wait to see them. It had been a weird and lonely summer.

I shifted my backpack from one shoulder to the other and stood on my toes, trying my best to see down the road.

"It's going to be a while longer," a voice behind me said. "Radio says there's a bit of an accident on the other side of town."

I turned to find an old man standing close to me. Uncomfortably close. He was barely an inch taller than me and wrapped in the itchiest-looking split pea soup–colored wool suit. His brown loafers were polished to a high shine, and his hair was slicked back in waves like a banker in a 1930s black-and-white film. He had a bulbous nose that had a bushy white mustache frothing out beneath it. His eyebrows were nearly invisible beneath the furrow of his brow, and teetering delicately on his nose, with no wires holding them behind his ears, were a pair of gold spectacles. He had a book in his hand with some paper sticking out.

He also looked entirely too old not to be taking advantage of the nearby bus stop bench.

"Geez, buddy! Where did you come from?" I said, stepping away from him discreetly. "If you want to sit down you can; I'm not using the bench."

Hopefully, he would take the hint.

"No, thank you, young lady," he said to my severe disappointment. "A man my age rests in one place too long, he never knows whether he's going to get back up again." He smiled cheerfully, his eyes crinkling at the sides.

We settled into silence for a moment, and I used looking down the street again as a way to put more precious inches between us. But the old man was undeterred.

"You seem to be someone used to waiting for buses," the man continued. "That doesn't quite sound like someone from around here."

"Buses are never on time no matter where you're from," I said dryly.

He let out a bark of a laugh. "Well spoken and very true. But I do think I may still be right. I beg your pardon if I'm prying, but I'm looking for someone in particular, and you do seem familiar."

I glanced at him again out of the corner of my eye but didn't move my head to face him. It was a trick I'd learned on the New York City trains. The more eye contact and attention you gave a complete stranger, the more they would continue to talk. If you didn't want to get involved, you just looked away and kept it that way. Before I moved to Hollow Falls, I could sit stock-still on the subway while a drunk man screamed two inches from my face. This wasn't much of a challenge in comparison.

"Mm-hmm," I said.

"Well!" the old man said with confidence. "I'm a mystery solver, so I'd better confront the challenge directly."

The phrase "mystery solver" piqued my interest, and I turned to meet his gaze.

The old man tucked his hands behind his back, like he was Sherlock Freakin' Holmes, and walked around me in a circle, looking me up and down.

"Let's see," he began. "I might be rusty, but I think your haircut is a bit too modern for Hollow Falls. I've seen the likes of it on television, but new fashions take an extra three years to get here, and you're here right now. And you have to be from somewhere that produces certain styles quicker than others because the color of your sweater hasn't had a home in youth fashion since 1988, so, like the hair, it must be fresh!" He nodded sharply in self-congratulation.

"As you know," he explained conspiratorially, "all things are cyclical—fashion included, my dear. Let's carry on. Your style makes it likely you've come from a big city. But not the West Coast, as you're dressed a bit more minimalist than they tend to.

"And you're headed north, and there isn't much retail north.

There are houses; it's residential. You've got a rather large bag with you, but it's not quite late enough in the day for a sleepover, so I doubt you're heading for a residence. Perhaps the school? You're the right age to be an attendant of Hollow Falls High. I'm an alumnus myself. But why the school when classes don't begin for nearly a week? And it's not quite three o'clock, which is far after school closes anyhow. Perhaps a club or activity that reconvenes early—the school paper would be my guess. Not the athletic type, are you?" He chuckled.

It was uncanny, but he was right. About all of it. It was very weird how many things he was able to pick out from my appearance to differentiate me from any other random teen in the town. I had been in the press recently, but stories about the Lit Killer hadn't included a picture of any of the students involved since we're all minors. Random townspeople shouldn't be able to get this close to figuring out who I was. Well. He *might* be able to recognize my voice from the podcast, but what was the point of him putting on this performance if he was a regular listener?

I took one step in the direction of school, having made the decision to bail on the bus and walk and wanting to use his moment of distraction for an escape.

"You must be Tig Torres!" he exclaimed, his eyes bursting open. "The bright young thing who got involved in the Lit

Killer case! And your city? New York, of course. You can't have moved here more than a year ago! Welcome to Hollow Falls. I've been looking all over for you."

I took an automatic step backward, in the direction of the school.

He opened his arms wide and bowed. "I am Mr. Green, and I have come to deliver to you . . . a package!"

Like a horrifically timed omen, the bus burst over the horizon and beeped loudly at Mr. Green to move back from the edge of the sidewalk. My opportunity to make a quick escape dissolved before my eyes. Now I'd be trapped on the same vehicle with him, potentially for the whole ride.

The old man shuffled as quickly as he could away from the curb, just in time for the bus to roll directly next to the space he had just vacated. The doors slammed open, and the bus driver glared at both of us. She definitely looked like she'd been held up on the other side of town: short of patience and sweaty with frustration.

"You coming or what?" she snapped.

"Oh, no, thank you, my dear. But this young lady has been waiting for some time, so I'm sure she's eager," he said politely, and turned back to me.

Mr. Green pushed a book and letter into my hands. "This little mystery is for you. There's a lot about this place waiting to be discovered and somehow . . . I feel like you'll be the one to get to the very bottom of it," he said with a wink.

Then Mr. Green waved at the bus driver and began hobbling slowly back down the sidewalk. I took the bus stairs in one giant leap, dug out one of those irritating fare tokens, and shoved it in the till, then packed myself in with the rest of the passengers who had been picked up on the delayed route.

As we rolled down the street, I watched Mr. Green duck into a large Victorian house at the end of the block. He'd barely had to leave his house to find me . . . I shivered and looked over my shoulder. I really hoped that I wasn't being watched.

The book in my hands was titled *Hollow Falls: A History* by Alan Mortimer Wyatt. The letter tucked inside had my full name written on it in spindly handwriting, curly like wedding calligraphy. Curious.

I glanced around the bus quickly. A woman a few seats up was peering nosily at me, and the old lady in the opposite aisle across from me was a gossipy neighbor of Abuela's. I frowned at the first woman until she turned away, and then tucked the book under my arm and out of view.

Clearly, this would have to wait until I got off the bus.

Chapter 2

Walking onto the school grounds felt eerie. It always does if you come after hours, on weekends, during summer break, or way too early in the morning. It's like visiting the house you grew up in, long after another family has moved in. The grass was still green, and the hallways smelled like they always did, but it still felt . . . hollow.

My heart began to beat a bit faster as I got closer to the *Talon* office, where Max, Wyn, and I had agreed to meet. I could hear muffled talking, which wasn't a surprise because I was definitely late.

I pushed open the door. Wyn and Max were there, just like I'd expected, but to my surprise Ella was there, too. I mean, I know she had helped us out during our hunt for the Lit Killer—and she even helped keep Max's faked death a secret—but I didn't realize she had been upgraded to a "hang outside of school" friend.

Although, perhaps hanging out was generous. Ella was sitting on top of a desk with her phone in her hand, looking exceedingly bored, while Wyn and Max were having some kind of heated argument. At the sound of the door banging against the wall, Wyn and Max both stopped shouting, and for a moment, everything was still.

Max had his bag in mid-swing, like he was getting ready to leave the room—the expression of irritation melting from his face. He had gotten a haircut, one that made his ears stick out a bit but made his eyes look bigger and sadder than I remembered. He was also taller and broader around the shoulders. It was startling how much he'd grown.

Ella was also a bit different from the last time I saw her. She was freckled and wearing surprisingly casual jean shorts and a T-shirt. Instead of her immaculate blowout, her hair was a riotous mass of ginger curls piled on her head in a scrunchie. She looked like a particularly glamorous camp counselor.

Wyn's white-blonde hair had gotten long and her skin brown from the sun of wherever she had vacationed. She seemed anxious, her hand dropping from where it had been reaching out to stop Max from leaving. For the first time since

I'd known her, she was wearing short sleeves. It took me longer than I'd admit to tear my eyes away.

"Tig!" Wyn shouted, and suddenly the arms I was staring at were around me tight as she collided against me with enough force to push the breath out of my chest.

"It's good to see you, too!" I laughed, patting her on the back.

Max crowded into the embrace, putting his chin directly on the top of my head. "You have no idea how boring it's been without you. Thank god you decided to show up."

"Yeah, yeah, I wouldn't miss this for the world!" I said, my words getting muffled in the expanse of his chest.

Ella shot me a quick smile over Max's shoulder and tucked her phone back into her purse.

"Nice to see you made it," she said. "I wish I could say the same for our stupid new adviser."

Adviser?

Max dropped his backpack onto the floor next to Wyn once our hug broke up. Wyn, looking a bit more flushed than usual, hopped up to sit on the desk next to Ella and folded her legs pretzel style. All the chairs were still stacked up for summer vacation. To my surprise, Ella didn't scoot over to give Wyn more room. They seemed strangely comfortable so close to each other. I guess I missed a lot this summer.

"I really am glad you made it," Wyn admitted. "I didn't know if you would want to help with the *Talon* this year, after . . . What I mean is, I would understand if you wanted to bail."

"Of course I was coming," I replied gently. "I wouldn't just leave you guys hanging. I've been looking forward to this, actually. And honestly? I'm ready for summer to be over."

"God. Same," Ella griped with an eye roll. "I fell asleep on the beach, and there's not going to be nearly enough time to fix my complexion before I have to start seeing actual people again."

Max pulled a chair from the stack and sat on it hard, primly swinging one leg over the other. "I feel that. I almost need a vacation from summer vacation," he said, waving his hand impatiently. "Plus, it's nice to be able to meet up with you guys again, after everything that happened, without it being on the first day of school. It . . . might have been too much to face the halls of this place while everyone was running and yelling—happy to be back—when the last thing I remember about being here was . . ." Max trailed off.

Wyn barked out a laugh. "Yeah, it still feels kind of gross sitting in this room and remembering Oly being here with us."

I had been trying not to think about Oly, but hearing Wyn say his name made a shiver go up my spine.

"Ugh, and speaking of he-who-must-not-be-named," Ella snapped. "We have to come up with some kind of social game plan for dealing with all the questions and weird looks. I'm sure the gossip mill is already winding up to go full tilt as soon as the first bell rings. People don't just brush off a bunch of deaths, a serial-killer teacher getting arrested, and his student protégé still on the loose like it's no big deal. And the four of us are ground zero when it comes to juicy details."

"Exactly, and besides all that," Max continued pointedly, "we need a happy, positive, front-page story for the *Talon* to draw some more people to join the paper when school starts. We can't make things weird for them just because our last newspaper adviser loved to murder and we're all 'traumatized.'" He put heavy finger quotes around the word. But you could tell from the tone of his voice that, deep down, he absolutely meant it. "It's going to be fun trying to get newbies to join a paper that was run by a serial killer. Even if Mr. Levinson is in jail now."

"Speaking of terrible advisers," Ella said, holding up her phone. "I just got an email from the new one. She was supposed to come to this meeting to kick things off and hand out assignments for the first issue, but she broke her arm or something. So she just emailed us some topics, and I guess we have to figure it out from there."

Ella sighed in exasperation. She opened her mail app and turned up her brightness so we could see the message better.

"We have to write a piece on Founder's Day?" Wyn scoffed with a grimace as she read. "God, that's so boring."

Even Max groaned and rubbed his eyes.

I must have been making a face because Ella shrugged.

"You came a little after the beginning of the school year last year, so you missed the last one," she said.

Max took his hands off his face and sighed loudly. "Basically, every September, the whole town does a treasure hunt to celebrate the founding of Hollow Falls. The mayor hides some little gold-painted treasure chest somewhere in town and makes up some riddles to help people find it. Whoever gets to it first gets a check for a hundred dollars and one of those gift baskets full of fruit or whatever," he explained.

"Everybody knows about Founder's Day already. This is like having to write a piece on the Fourth of July."

"Hmm," Ella said.

"What?" Wyn griped. "Don't tell me you're actually interested in this puff piece?"

Ella shrugged. "There's a little bit more to its history than most people know. I overheard my dad talking about it with his weird Murder of Crows friends when I was a kid. They never thought I was listening, but I always was."

"Well? We're waiting. Spill," Max said impatiently.

"Fine, fine," Ella said with a grin. "How much do you know about The Hunt?"

Max, Wyn, and I looked at one another blankly, then waited for Ella to continue.

Ella preened, clearly pleased with the attention, and settled in to tell the story. "Apparently, after the town founder died under mysterious circumstances, he was buried in secret by his closest confidants, and they buried a treasure along with him. They decided to put together a puzzle that could only be solved by the exact sort of person who deserved the treasure. Someone inquisitive, careful, mindful, and well read. The people who made it their mission to find the founder and his treasure dubbed it The Hunt. And no one has found it in a hundred and seventy years."

"Huh," Max said, crossing his arms, curious.

"That's cool and all, but what does it have to do with Founder's Day?" I asked.

"Oh, duh. Anyway, people were getting so thirsty for The Hunt that people started getting killed. So they created some family-friendly scavenger hunt in the 1970s, rebranded it as Founder's Day, and hoped everyone would lose interest in the real treasure."

"What kind of puzzle is it?" I asked.

Ella sighed. "It's just more stupid riddles. Apparently the historical ones we have in the library right now are just the first two, but there were originally six. The remaining riddles were destroyed and all references to them were removed from the town records to prevent people from finding them."

She sighed again. "I hate riddles; they're the most boring kind of puzzle."

"Let's agree to disagree," I replied dryly. I looked down at my hands and realized I was still holding the book the old man had given me at the bus stop: *Hollow Falls: A History*.

"Speaking of our town's weird origins," I said, waving the book at my friends. "Some spooky old man accosted me in the street on my way here and told me there's some mystery I need to get to the bottom of."

"Way to bury the lede!" Wyn interrupted. "What kind of spooky was he? Regular spooky or Hollow Falls spooky?"

"Definitely Hollow Falls spooky," I said, clutching the book and letter a bit tighter. "I was waiting for the bus *forever,* and I was about ready to bail and just walk. But before I lost my patience completely, this old man wanders up and starts talking at me. And I am not kidding when I mean *at* me. He says he thinks he can guess who I am and is being really suspicious—"

"Like dangerous suspicious?" Wyn interjected again.

"Not exactly. He seemed too old to be dangerous," I

explained. "He was the kind of old where if I knocked into him accidentally, I'm pretty sure he would just fall over and shatter. He was like 1970s Willy Wonka spooky—like the kind of guy who would own a lot of taxidermy."

"Gross," Ella said with a shudder. I could only imagine she was remembering the dead animal collection we'd found in Levinson's murder cabin.

"What happened next?" Max asked, leaning forward, eager for me to continue.

"So, he walks around me a bunch and then starts rattling off weirdo observations about my hair and clothes. Then, just when the bus drove up, the old man announces that he had been looking for me specifically, and he shoved this book with a letter inside into my hands."

I placed them both on the desk.

"What did the letter say?" Max asked, picking it up.

"I don't know, I haven't opened it yet."

Before I was even finished talking, Wyn tore open the envelope and shook the paper out. A key dropped out with it and bounced on the linoleum with a clang.

"Oh, wow . . ." Wyn said, reading. "This is . . . wow."

"Would you please actually read it out loud?" Max said, snatching the key off the ground.

"Hold your horses, Maximillian," Wyn huffed.

Dearest Miss Torres,

We would like to extend a formal invitation to this month's meeting of the Murder of Crows, a venerable society dedicated to the preservation and analysis of Hollow Falls's history and mystery. We were very impressed with your work concerning the Lit Killer and would love to hear all about the dashing derring-do, if you were so inclined to share. As you know, our membership was very affected by the situation, and we would like to share in the tale as a form of closure. In return, we would love to extend to you our own knowledge and the fellowship of mystery within our town.

For a sleuth like yourself, our treasure trove of a library may turn out to be an indispensable resource. One well deserved for a person who saved us from the killer in our midst.

We will be meeting tonight, Friday the 17th, at 8:00 p.m. sharp. In this envelope, you will find a key to the door of the building in which we'll be meeting and a map to our location. You are allowed to bring only one guest.

Best of luck, and we hope to see you and hear about your wonderful work in person.

Yours,
Alan Mortimer Wyatt

"Cool that there's a secret library. But it smells like he sprayed it with old-man perfume," Wyn continued. She handed me back the letter, and I turned it over to find an unlabeled map, with a crow marking the spot. A little on the nose, but I respected their commitment.

"Mysterious," Max said. "I figured the Murder of Crows had disbanded after the whole Lit Killer thing was over. Why on earth would they want to keep hanging out when one of their own turned out to be a wackadoodle, killing their members left and right? If I loved murder but didn't want to be murdered, I would just go home, put on some *Forensic Files*, and call it a day."

"I don't know why they're still meeting, Max, but I'd like to find out," I said firmly. I thought about the last time we'd encountered the Murder of Crows. Their obstruction of justice in the Lit Killer case still left a bad taste in my mouth, but I guess I couldn't blame them for not expecting the call to be coming from inside the house, so to speak. Maybe this was some kind of apology.

"So . . . you guys in? Are we going to do this?" I asked, holding out my hand to take the key back from Max.

Wyn shrugged. "We have two weeks before school starts. What else do we have going on? And who knows? Maybe we could even ask around at the meeting and dig up some dirt on The Hunt to make this Founder's Day article a little more interesting." There was a mischievous glint in her eyes.

"I'm out." Ella shook her head. "My dad used to take me along to those meetings all the time when I was a kid. I've had enough of Old Man Wyatt's giant dumb house for a lifetime."

Ella paused and then shot me a sickly sweet smile. "You'll probably have a great time, though, Tig. It's right up your alley."

I didn't dignify her with a response.

"I'm going to sit the meeting out, too," Max chimed in. "I'm trying a new thing called being careful. You guys can be on the front line for this one. We need another couple stories just to bulk up the paper anyway. So while you guys handle your own dark twist on the Founder's Day assignment, I'm going to cover the reopening of the Montague Hotel. I'm sure at least some of the students will want to know if the renovations are going to be completed before prom night."

"And I'll do the actual fluff work and fill in a gossip column or something," Ella said with a shrug. "That's basically already my job here anyway."

"Well, I'm game for tagging along to the meeting," Wyn said. "It looks like we have a date, Torres."

My cheeks heated against my control. "Thanks, Wyn," I said, my voice absolutely not cracking. "Even though this Mr. Wyatt guy seems weirdly fixated on me specifically, we worked together to solve the Lit Killer case. Like hell I'm going to soak up all the credit for solving that case alone."

"You better not, you nerd," Wyn teased with a grin, gently hip-checking me to the side. "Now we just have to figure out this map."

"Oh, it's that creeptastic house up at the north end of Minute Street. It has a bunch of crows on it; you'll know it when you see it," Ella said casually, sliding off the desk. "Work smart, not hard.

"And since our adviser isn't here to tell me no, I'm heading out early. I'll see you guys later. Have fun hanging out with my dad and his old folks' Goth retirement club."

Ella swung her purse over her shoulder and flounced out the door.

Now that we had the location, this all seemed a bit more real. I wondered whether the Murder of Crows was expecting a whole detailed presentation or if it would be more like a Q&A. I'd never really presented a case before, and the thought was a bit nerve-racking.

"What are you planning to wear?" Wyn asked casually. "Business casual? Cocktail? Black tie?"

"I was planning to wear this," I said, looking down at my T-shirt and jeans.

Wyn pursed her lips. "It's a presentation, and a mysterious

one. Might be a good idea to leave some kind of impression. Especially if we're attending as representatives of the *Talon.*"

I scoffed. "Well, I'll wear a dress if you wear a dress," I shot back, ending that line of conversation.

Wyn looked me up and down with a peculiar look in her eye and smirked.

"Annnnnd Wyn's chosen the dress," Max said with a huff. "You have no idea what you've just gotten yourself into, Tig."

"Hmm." Wyn picked her bag up from the floor. "Someone has a speech to write, so we should probably get out of here. I'll see you at seven fifty." Wyn pulled open the door, blew us a kiss (which was somehow both sarcastic and very, very cute), and then disappeared into the hallway.

"You should wear something nice, or she's going to outshine you," Max said dryly. He handed *Hollow Falls: A History* back to me and picked his own backpack up off the ground.

"Wyn?" I said incredulously, thinking about her normal cool grunge gear.

"I've known her for a long time." Max tightened the strap on his pack with jerky finality. "Wear something nice."

Chapter 3

I fidgeted in my ill-fitting black dress pants, pulling them down to cover more of my ankles. I wasn't in the habit of collecting business-casual clothing, so half of last year's Christmas church outfit would have to do. The pants had gotten way too short, but like hell was Wyn going to cave and wear a dress, so neither would I. I almost bailed on the fancy clothes completely, but after some thought, I realized that Wyn was definitely right about it being important to make a good impression. Regardless of their intentions or hobbies, some of the most influential adults in the whole town had at some point been members of the Murder of Crows. There was nothing more irritating than being treated like a child in adult spaces, and not dressing like one usually helped a bit.

When the bus pulled up to the Minute Street stop, I adjusted my bag on my shoulder—stuffed with the articles and presentation supplies I had brought—and made my way down the stairs and toward the Murder of Crows headquarters.

The crow-covered house at 3141 N. Minute Street had a large, ivy-covered wrought-iron gate with the club's symbol right in the center—ostentatious and not secretive at all. There was a long, sprawling path up to the front door. I could see the white blonde of Wyn's hair through the thick foliage, which made me feel a lot better about pushing the gate open. She was sitting a bit behind one of the pillars on the porch. I recognized the cuffs and bracelets around her wrist as she played with her phone, but the heels were *new*. Completely out-of-character new. Double-take, then triple-take new. I tugged my pants down yet again and cursed, thinking about Max's words earlier.

"Glad to see you made it," Wyn called from behind the pillar. "I was about to consider taking a long walk up the street to find you."

I huffed as I jogged along the path and up the front stairs, clutching my bag in front of me. "We have three more minutes until the meeting starts," I began. "They should be glad we made it on time at all! Whoa, what? Whoa!"

I stared; I couldn't help it. Wyn stood and smoothed her hand down the side of her dress slowly. It was a devastatingly simple black pencil dress, elegantly cut like nothing I had ever seen anyone in this town approximate, even on their very best days. Sleeves down to her elbows, subtle boning in the bodice, hem two inches below her knee so that the fabric stretched between her hips. Her messy, fluffy blonde hair was brushed back into a slick French twist, as severe as it was sophisticated. The chipped black nail polish on her hands had been replaced with a delicate dusty rose that had to have been borrowed from someone else in her house. It was such an alien color to see on Wyn that it took a full ten seconds to tear my eyes away from it.

"It's my mom's," Wyn explained. She raised an eyebrow at my expression and leaned one hip against the wood pillar. "She used to walk runway for Thierry Mugler in the '90s and has a lot of this shit lying around the basement. I usually trot it out once a year to hurt people. Mostly Ella if I'm being honest."

"Yeah, I . . . uh . . . I see how this would make Ella sweat a bit," I said, semi-hysterically. "Should I have worn something fancier?"

Wyn laughed, and the illusion was shattered with the familiar crinkling of her nose. "Not at all, bro. You just said, '*I'll* wear a dress if *you* wear a dress,' like you didn't think

I could. And I just figured I should let you know that I can."

Wyn tilted her head and looked down at me through her eyelashes. "If I'm going to be honest, the shoes hurt like a bitch and my hair is too tight. But it was worth it to see the look on your face." Her gaze softened a bit.

"We all contain multitudes, Tig. You should see how Max cleans up when he's really given a moment and place to shine. Gay Excellence, that one."

And with that, Wyn stepped across the porch and grabbed the large brass knocker. The noise was so startling that I almost dropped my bag.

"You look really good—even if you bailed on the dress," Wyn said gently. "Just take a deep breath and be yourself."

So, I took a deep breath, and the door opened. An older woman with a sharp, asymmetrical gray haircut opened the door. She looked both of us up and down, with an arch expression. "Huh. I'm surprised you showed up. Welcome to the Murder of Crows, Tig Torres," she said dryly, her voice deep and resonant. She met my eyes and examined me with a look I couldn't quite figure out—it was almost resentful, but also kind of sad. I looked away quickly. If the rest of the Murder of Crows gave off the same vibes, we were in for a long evening.

"The auditorium is at the end of this hall and to the right," she continued. "No recording equipment can be used on the premises." The woman turned around, the drapey fringed shawl she wore across her shoulders sweeping in a wide arc behind her. "I can't *wait* to hear what you have to say." She smirked and sauntered down the hall.

I raised my eyebrows at Wyn as we stepped into the foyer. "Odd choice for the welcoming committee," I muttered. Wyn chuckled as she closed the door behind her, and then we both gasped when we finally turned around and got a load of the house. The space sprawled before us like a museum. The floors were dark wood with an intricate mosaic that matched the symbols and whorls of the wrought-iron fence from outside. The walls were densely decorated with framed oil paintings, technical diagrams, and painstakingly preserved newspaper clippings. There was a long black carpet that stretched from the front door all the way to the end of the hallway, where the woman who had opened the door for us had disappeared.

"Tig, what the hell is this house?" Wyn asked.

I gazed up at the huge chandelier above the entryway, its red crystals glinting coldly in the light.

"It reminds me of the Diogenes Club," I said.

"The what?" Wyn asked.

"The Diogenes Club from Sherlock Holmes," I clarified. "Look at all the Murder of Crows logos around here. I can't believe someone lives here. Everything's so fancy. I don't know how to function around rich people," I theater-whispered.

"I don't know," Wyn said. "I feel like with the shoes I blend right in. See?"

Wyn tossed her head back and pulled an exaggerated snobbish expression, then sashayed down the hallway.

"Oh my god, stop," I hissed after her.

"Make me," Wyn tossed over her shoulder with a grin as she put one foot directly in front of the other, her hips swinging from side to side, a stunning replica of a runway strut. Before she reached the end of the hallway, where the open door to the meeting room was, she turned on her heel, dropped her shoulder, and posed.

"Get back over here!" I whisper-shrieked.

Wyn guffawed and kicked off her heels and tucked them under her arm. With a quick glance at the open door, she dashed back down the hallway in her stockings, sliding the last few feet until she hit the welcome mat and caught herself against the front door.

"Oh my god, Wyn, what if someone saw you?" I said with a laugh.

"What if they did?" Wyn said, putting her shoes down neatly in the corner. "They're probably just glad we came. Besides, now you're not anxious about your big speech."

I sighed. "You're right, you're right. It did help a bit."

Wyn held out her hand and led me to the meeting room barefoot, and something in my chest warmed up and settled a little.

As we got farther down the hallway, we could hear voices and the clinking of glasses. We stepped into the auditorium, which appeared to be a large, three-story dining room that had been converted into a lecture hall, both much grander and much smaller than I had assumed it would be. As we came through the French doors, Mr. Green pushed through the small crowd to greet us—much more warmly than the woman who had opened the door.

"It's wonderful to see you, my dear, and what a lovely guest you've brought! You must be Wyn Abbott. I'd recognize that vivacious spirit anywhere!" Mr. Green exclaimed, reaching out to shake both our hands. "Everyone will get settled in a moment, and you can start at the front of the room near the large armchair. There is a seat for your guest near the front in case she has anything to add to the presentation."

Mr. Green patted the top of my hand, gave a short polite bow, and went to find his seat. The auditorium was arranged with a large table at the back, with drinks and a few platters of sliced fruit and cheese. There was seating for at least thirty people: wood chairs arranged in a semicircle, crowding around the large emerald-green tufted armchair at the front of the room. To either side of the armchair were two smaller armchairs in brown leather, almost like the seating was meant for a panel. The guests were already beginning to settle into the audience space, and the room was getting quieter as they waited for me to begin.

I pulled the maps, newspaper clippings, and photographs out of my bag and set them in a neat pile at the foot of the chair. I took a moment to look at the members. There were some people I recognized—like Ella's dad, Mayor Eldridge Highsmith, and the town librarian. But there were also a lot of strangers, emphasis on the strange. Like a tall woman dressed head to toe in white, with eyebrows and hair bleached to match, and a set of twins who had serious *The Shining* energy.

But even more odd, across the room, roughly twenty-five feet from the ground, was a medium-sized cutout in the wall. Through the opening, there was an old man dressed in a gray robe peering down at the festivities. I squinted up at him, but he was too far away to recognize and he was holding some kind of looking glass in front of his face while watching the crowd. Then, suddenly, he swung the glass in my direction and raised a hand in greeting. I gasped involuntarily. *What the hell was this place?*

But before I could question it further, Mr. Green cleared his throat and stood up, opening his arms wide to address the crowd.

"Friends and enemies, and those without designation," he said, his eyes twinkling, "we have a treat tonight. Quite recently, our little town—and more specifically, our little group—was rocked with a series of gruesome murders, clever as they were cruel. As we trembled among one another, the foundations of our fraternity shaken by the bloodstained hands of our betrayer, our town's clever young minds were hard at work. Facing danger and disaster, they refused to bow beneath the horror. Tonight, their leader is here to tell the tale of how they faced the Lit Killer and emerged from his clutches victorious. I would like to introduce you all to the incandescent Tig Torres."

The crowd clapped, and I squared my shoulders.

"Good evening," I began. "I would like to thank Mr. Green for inviting me and Wyn to your meeting."

I faltered as the crowd stared back at me in expectation. This was somehow much harder and much worse than presenting a class project at school.

"As Mr. Green said, my name is Tig Torres and I'll be speaking to you all about my experience with the Lit Killer."

Finally, some of the members of the audience leaned forward

in interest, and more than one opened a notebook—their pens poised to take notes. A serious audience was hard, but a curious one? I could work with that.

"You know when you see something and it's not quite right? When a solution seems too convenient, almost to the point where it's insulting? Then you get that feeling that nags in the back of your brain like a tangle of yarn that needs to be picked at.

"Well, everything about the Lit Killer was miles of string, snarled over itself and pulled tight—into patterns in some places and knots in others. I couldn't just let it be. And from what I've been led to believe, I don't think any of you would have, either."

I got up from the armchair and picked up the first of my documents, holding it up for the audience to see.

"This is Beth Torres, the Lit Killer's favorite victim: an investigator who got so close to solving the mystery that she paid with her life. She was also the patsy the police blamed for the Lit Killer's murders—and she was my aunt. From the instant I stepped into this town, I knew that I had to avenge her death by bringing the real killer to justice . . . because no one else would."

When I finished telling my story, several members dashed up from their seats to ask questions as Wyn and I gathered the disorganized papers from the presentation that were littered in front of the armchair.

"That was wonderful, Tig! Thank you so much for your time!" Mr. Green swanned in. He placed a friendly hand on my forearm so he could tug me a few feet away from the din. "The way you handled all that darkness was . . . impeccable. We're very lucky to have you in our little town."

"Thank you, Mr. Green, I'm glad you liked it," I said, looking over my shoulder at Wyn. She had taken the opportunity to launch into more details with some of the members who were looking up at her in awe and fascination.

"What would be even luckier is if you were interested in accepting an invitation to be a more familiar face around these parts," he said a bit more quietly.

"What?" I turned back to him, confused.

"We would like to offer you membership . . . to the Murder of Crows," Mr. Green clarified. "You're an exceptional young detective, and your grasp of the bigger picture is exquisite. A lot of our members are getting older, and we'd love to invite more young people like yourself to keep this tradition alive. We have resources that would—"

"I'm so sorry, Mr. Green," I interrupted him. "But I'm

going to have to decline. I just have a lot going on right now, you know?"

Mr. Green looked disappointed.

"But it's not that I wouldn't love to attend maybe sometime in the future?" I said quickly.

He closed his eyes and shook his head; then, smiling, he patted my hand once again. "Oh, you don't have to let me down easy. I'm grown-up enough for bad news. I appreciate the gesture, though. And our offer to use our library still stands, independent of membership."

I nodded and smiled, glad he seemed to be comfortable with my answer.

"I hope you'll stay and look around, have some refreshments. The first floor is entirely open to guests; however, I must ask that you refrain from going upstairs. These old walls are filled with so many secrets. We can't have a detective like you figuring them all out!"

Mr. Green gave me one last short bow and a wink and stepped away to join another group.

I saw a flash out of the corner of my eye as Mr. Green walked away. It was the old man in the cutout window above the auditorium. He waited until he was sure I was looking, and then he slowly and pointedly gestured for me to come up before he disappeared again.

Wyn caught my eye from across the room, where the crowd around her had finally dispersed. She cocked her eyebrow in question, and I grinned in response, jerking my head toward the door.

Maybe this evening wouldn't be so boring after all.

Chapter 4

As we left the auditorium, I got Wyn up to speed about the man in the window and Mr. Green's warning to stay on the first floor—a suggestion we were obviously going to ignore.

We roamed the hallways, looking for an opportunity to sneak upstairs, but so far, we kept getting interrupted by other MOC members.

After my speech, the majority of the club members had split into smaller subgroups and headed to their own corner of the house. It appeared that while the Murder of Crows was a large group, individuals had their own projects or reading groups within it. It was beginning to become easier for me to understand how the Lit Killer had both thrived and flown under the radar here. Constantly surrounded by a community of his peers, he had an excellent resource of potential victims. But, as Mr. Green had said "friends and enemies" when he introduced me, clearly not all the Lit Killer's peers were automatically allies.

Every time we made a break for the stairs, someone else wandered by for a drink refill or to chat with another member or to ask us more questions about the Lit Killer. Which left me and Wyn standing aimlessly in the hallway, twisting locked door handles and trying to look casual.

"We have to find a way upstairs. That dude was *old*," I hissed at Wyn as yet another murder groupie wandered by. "What if he dies before we make it up there?"

"I'll take you."

I whirled around. Leaning against the staircase railing a few feet away was a guy about our age. He was wearing a red windbreaker, had a camera around his neck, and had soft, floppy blond hair falling into his eyes. Even though he couldn't have been older than his late teens, his hair was shot through with gray and he looked tired, the underneath of his eyes dark and bruised. Wyn scowled at him immediately but said nothing.

"I'm surprised you didn't just go up on your own, Tig Torres. Rules be damned. As a fan of your work, I expected a bit more from you."

"Uh, am I supposed to know who you are or something?" I asked.

He shrugged. "We went to the same school for a bit, actually. I graduated this spring from Hollow Falls High. Judah Beckett, at your service. Nice to see you here, too, Wyn."

Wyn scoffed, and Judah rubbed the back of his neck sheepishly. "Okay, looks like you're still mad . . ." he said.

Wyn huffed, then turned to me. "Judah was the editor of the *Talon* the year before you got here. When I tried to join back in freshman year, he pressured the rest of the paper to lock me out. I had to wait until he literally quit."

"In my defense, you didn't seem like you were that serious about writing," Judah shot back. "And you were always in detention after school, which is when we usually met anyway."

He paused, then shrugged. "I'm not too stubborn to admit I was wrong, though. You do good work, and you have a strong understanding of editing and format. The paper is absolutely in good hands now that all the older editors have graduated and Mr. Levinson isn't lurking around every corner. Between you, Tig, and that other weird kid, the *Talon* is giving some of the real local papers a run for their money."

Wyn, who had clearly been charging up for an argument, pinked gently in surprise. "Oh. Well. Thank you," she replied, clearly thrown off balance.

Judah gave her a small smile, then turned to me.

"You were more of a sharp left hook to the paper. Unexpected and powerful. Your podcast is the best thing that's happened around here in a while. I've been hoping to run into you more organically, but beggars can't be choosers, I guess.

"I'm actually working on a project that I'd love to talk to you about sometime. I left the paper to work on a novel about the town and its particular . . . particularities. It would be great to go over it with someone who sees things with fresh, inquisitive eyes. I'm sure you've noticed that things are a bit creepy around here . . . Anyway, do you mind if we exchange contact info?"

I glanced over at Wyn—she was the one who had beef with him, so she would know if this was a bad idea or not—but she just shrugged.

"Uh, sure," I decided, pulling out my phone.

Judah handed over his own, and we tapped our details into each other's contacts. He sent a quick *Hey* with a little bat emoji to confirm.

"Now that we're friends—acquaintances," Judah corrected quickly at Wyn's arched eyebrow, "let me show you upstairs to the library and our esteemed host."

He gestured for us to follow him up the stairs. As soon as we reached the second-floor landing, the din of the other club members disappeared, and the light faded until it was barely enough to see five feet ahead of us. The halls were much narrower than downstairs—only wide enough for two people to stand next to each other. And the carpet was so plush that it silenced our footsteps.

"What's he like . . . Mr. Wyatt?" I asked softly as we turned a corner to go up yet another dark flight of stairs.

"He's a good guy. A little histrionic, but half the old people here are like that anyway," Judah replied, stopping at the landing. "You're almost there. It's just at the end of that hallway. I would come and introduce you, but frankly, I don't want to get trapped in a long conversation. You know how boomers are."

"You've got that right." Wyn huffed. "Don't worry, we can find our way from here."

Judah gave a cocky salute and a wry grin, then disappeared down into the gloom. The end of the hallway was a bit brighter, as the library door was framed on either side with sconces. We knocked softly but no one answered, so I pushed the door open and walked into the room.

It was about the size of the sitting room downstairs, with bookshelves lining all the walls. There were standing shelves arranged in rows with a main walkway down the middle of them leading to a large table that was piled with books. Behind the table was a giant chalkboard on the wall with sweeping patterns across it that suggested it was wiped clean in a hurry.

The shelves were filled with books (obviously), but in the center of each wall shelf was a space that was cleared for artifacts—from rocks to animal teeth and feather samples, and even a stunning display of what appeared to be raw silver, raw gold, sulfur, and something else chunky and crystalline. Each specimen had a date, name, and location within the city on the identification card below it.

I took a closer look at the books lining the shelf in front of me and pulled one out at random. It was about Hollow Falls. I turned to the shelf behind me and picked up another book. *Hollow Falls: A History.* The same book Mr. Green had given me at the bus stop.

"I think this is a library of the city," I said, looking around the space again. "I'm willing to bet all the animal stuff is samples from every single animal that lives within city limits, and the rock wall is probably all the types of rock that are in the region. And that last wall with the gold and silver might be soil samples or something."

Wyn pulled out a long drawer that had been artfully placed along the length of the table.

"Oh, cool. There's a bunch of maps."

She reached in, then paused before touching anything, rethinking her actions. Spotting a pair of white cloth gloves on the table, she put them on and then lifted one of the maps from the drawer.

I grinned. "I'm sure whoever owns them will appreciate that."

But before Wyn could explore the maps any further, we heard a loud creak from the opposite corner of the room. We turned just in time to see one of the shelves swing open, revealing a messy office space hidden behind the wall.

Papers were strewn everywhere, sweaters and coats were draped over an armchair, and stacks of books were scattered throughout the cramped space, all of them leaning dubiously. And in the middle of the mess, directly across from me and Wyn, was a very tall old man. The man from the window.

He reached out to shake my hand.

"Tig Torres. It's wonderful to meet you, my dear. Thank you for accepting my invitation. I'm Alan Mortimer Wyatt."

Chapter 5

Alan Mortimer Wyatt was built like a man who in his youth had been incredibly powerful. I could see the ghosts of muscles in his broad shoulders and the memory of a once-rugged chin on his ancient face. He wasn't dressed like he was about to attend a party being thrown in his own house at all—instead wearing button-down pajamas and the plush gray robe that I'd glimpsed from downstairs. Mr. Wyatt motioned for us to join him in his hidden office and sat heavily in the leather chair behind his desk after shaking our hands.

"Your speech was beautifully delivered," Mr. Wyatt continued. "I can't thank you enough for helping us remove the jackal from within our midst. We are a gaggle of oddities to be sure, but there is a line between enthusiasm and method acting, if you know what I mean."

"Thank you for having us," I replied graciously. "Your home and library are both incredible."

"Yes, thank you," Wyn echoed.

Mr. Wyatt glowed with pleasure but waved his big hand in dismissal. "Oh, you flatterer. It's not all my work. The best things are a group effort."

He was different from what I'd expected based on his letter and what I knew about the Murder of Crows. I'd built him up in my head as a mysterious benefactor, but he mostly just felt like someone's grandpa. But I still got the sense he—and his club—were hiding something. That he had invited me here tonight for more than just a public speaking engagement. Why else would he invite us up here against Mr. Green's explicit instructions to remain on the first floor?

I decided to test the waters on my theory. "So why didn't you come down and join the group—if you don't mind me asking?"

"I don't get down all these stairs that much these days," he explained quietly. "When you're my age, you choose a room you like best and you stay in it." He chuckled softly and held up a pair of delicate opera glasses.

"Those are so cool!" Wyn said.

"If you think *those* are 'cool,' I have something else that might interest you both," Mr. Wyatt said, arranging his mobility aids and shooing us toward the door. "It wouldn't do to leave a party without souvenirs."

We followed him out into the library. Once we were back in the shelf-lined room, Mr. Wyatt looked at us both seriously. "I must admit, I did have a bit of an ulterior motive, asking you here tonight, Tig."

I couldn't stop a smile from crawling across my face. *I knew it.*

"I know it's a bit bold of me to come to you for anything after you've already provided such an exemplary service to our community," he continued, leaning heavily on his walker. "However, it is precisely because you have proven yourself in this way that I believe you would be an incredible asset to the task I must ask of you."

He pulled a book from one of the shelves, then walked slowly over to the large table.

"Now, I'm sure Mr. Green asked you if you would like to join the Murder of Crows and it's my best guess that you said no?" he asked.

"Yeah . . . I mean no offense—" I started, but Mr. Wyatt put up a gentle hand.

"None taken. The old bat had to try. You don't seem like the club-joining type to me. You've got independence in your eyes."

To my surprise, Wyn piped up. "She works with me, Max, and sometimes Ella," she said to Mr. Wyatt, then turned to me, as if for confirmation.

Mr. Wyatt nodded and reached up to pluck a book off the shelf behind the desk.

"Smaller teams get more done, I agree." He wiped the book he was holding down with a small cloth, then handed it to me.

"Thank you," I said politely, unclear what yet another old book had to do with this mysterious task he had for me. Would it kill these old guys to just come out with it already?

"Open it, open it!" he urged gently.

The title of the book was *The History and Mystery of Hollow Falls*. The cover of the book was brown and worn, but its pages were edged with gold. When I peeled back the first few sheets, I was surprised to find that the book had been hollowed out. Inside was a beautiful antique spyglass. I lifted it up to the light, then brought one end to my eye.

"This is too much, Mr. Wyatt," I said haltingly. "I mean, don't get me wrong—it's very cool. But you don't have to give me a gift for solving the Lit Killer case. It was sort of my life's mission after all." I suddenly felt awkward. I didn't mean to get so real with this old dude I just met.

Mr. Wyatt crossed his arms and leaned back against the table. "My dear, you saved our lives. This token is simply the least I can do," he said, soft and honest. "When you came to visit us the first time and managed to unravel our own dangerous mystery, I knew I had to arrange for you to come and receive this in person as a symbol of my gratitude."

Mr. Wyatt smiled, but it didn't reach his eyes. Instead, he seemed a bit sad. "This," he continued, "is a gift, but it's also an opportunity. A spyglass is a tool that helps to reveal what cannot be seen with the eyes alone. I'm sure when the time is right you'll find it to be absolutely invaluable." His words were laced with meaning I didn't quite understand.

"Can I see?" Wyn asked.

I handed the spyglass to her.

"Keep it close and protect it," Mr. Wyatt said urgently. "This is a gift for you and your band of sleuths and no one else. Keep it from getting into the wrong hands. I didn't put it in a hollowed-out book for nothing."

Wyn handed the spyglass back, and I tucked it gently inside its literary safe house. Wyn looked at the book's cover closely. "Mr. Wyatt," she said slowly. "We're working on a story for the paper about Founder's Day, and we heard that the Murder of Crows has a history with the event." She paused. "And with something called The Hunt."

Mr. Wyatt looked startled, and he leaned heavily against the table. "Well, you young people are even more intuitive than I gave you credit for. The Hunt is precisely why I asked you to come here today."

Wyn and I both gasped, and Wyn took a large step backward.

"Yes, the Murder of Crows was integral to the Founder's Day celebration you all know so well. Back in the 1970s, we worked together with the mayor to shut The Hunt down. It was a bloodbath."

"Oh my god." I fumbled my recorder out of my pocket and turned it on, house rules be damned. "Can you talk to us about it?"

"That's why you're here, isn't it?" Mr. Wyatt sighed. It seemed like by confiding in us, he was crossing his own personal Rubicon. I was dying to know why this old-timey scavenger hunt had people so riled up.

After a pause that felt like eons, Mr. Wyatt continued, "Transforming The Hunt into a holiday wasn't a particularly hard decision, although it didn't go over well with everyone. Things had gotten very out of hand at that point, and the mayor at the time practically jumped at our idea for Founder's Day. It only took a generation for most people in town to forget about The Hunt or to grow too old to keep looking," he said, gazing off into the distance.

"Before it came to that, I was a young hotshot with

something to prove, and Mr. Green was my right-hand man. We were so terribly deep into The Hunt that neither of us even went to university until after everything had been settled. Everyone was invested in finding the founder's body and the treasure that was rumored to come with it. There was urbane criminal activity, hooligans were digging up graves and destroying public property, and people were getting hurt—and killed. When the scent of incredible fortune is waved at the noses of bloodhounds, they do what they were bred to do. The day The Hunt became more about avoiding death than the thrill of the search, the exchange was no longer worth it. One day, I woke up and I'd just had enough. Sofia will tell you."

"Sofia—like my abuela Sofia?" I questioned.

Mr. Wyatt looked surprised. "Of course. Doesn't she know you're here?"

"No . . ." I admitted begrudgingly. "I took the bus. She'll be sorry she missed you. If I'd known you two knew each other, I would have asked her to tag along."

Mr. Wyatt smiled sadly. "I haven't seen Sofia for quite some time. Since . . . Well, it doesn't matter, does it? The past is the past."

"But what hap—"

"One story at a time," Mr. Wyatt interrupted. He shook his head as if to clear his thoughts before starting again.

"Despite the Founder's Day tradition, there are still factions of people who have kept The Hunt alive all these years, in whispers and dark corners. Many of them are members of this very club. Not all of them are friends, and all of them have their own motives, as I once did.

"I have spent my life in search of the founder's body and its treasure. The Hunt is a part of my legacy. I couldn't bear to see it fall into the hands of people who don't understand its worth."

I noticed that he was leaning heavily on the table, so I pushed a nearby chair behind him and he settled into it gratefully.

"Thank you, dear." He took a deep breath. "This is where you and your friends come in, Tig Torres. I'm sure The Hunt was intended for good purposes, but this whole situation has brought so much strife and pain to the community. The holiday is just a Band-Aid on a broken arm.

"I'm an old man, and I would like to see this whole matter put to rest before I'm gone. I'd like you to help me find the founder's body and have the treasure—whatever it may be—either distributed among the townspeople or preserved in the library or museum."

Mr. Wyatt sounded worried, but his words filled me with a thrill. A real treasure hunt with a dark history! Mystery players with secret motives and a generation of elders with adventurous pasts to hide.

Wyn caught my eye over Mr. Wyatt's shoulder and raised her eyebrows excitedly.

"So . . . where do we start?" I asked.

"First, we—" Mr. Wyatt began, but before he could finish, the door to the library burst open with a crash.

Chapter 6

My head whipped toward the door at the opposite end of the library. Standing in its shadow, looking suspiciously back at us, was a stocky man in a very nice suit. He was in his early fifties, his wavy hair combed down and pomaded to a bright shine.

"What are you talking about?" he asked rudely.

Mr. Wyatt closed his eyes for a second, then gestured to the man.

"Franklin Baker, Tig and Wyn. Tig and Wyn, Franklin Baker," Mr. Wyatt said.

Franklin pinched his lips into a thin line, his eyes raking us up and down fiercely.

"What are they doing in here?" he demanded. His hand on the doorknob tightened until his knuckles were white.

"Nothing that concerns you," Mr. Wyatt replied archly. "This is *my* home after all. But if you must know, I was thanking Tig for her speech this evening. Is there something I can help you with, Mr. Baker?"

"As a matter of fact, there is," he said smarmily. "Mr. Green got a cake." He jerked his head at me dismissively. "He was looking for them. They need to come downstairs immediately."

"Why?" I said placidly. It wasn't really a question. I don't take orders from strange men.

Franklin Baker spluttered furiously, as if no one had ever defied him before.

Mr. Wyatt rolled his eyes. "Don't go for his sake, but I'd love to have a slice of that cake if you girls don't mind. Bring me up a piece when you're done?"

"No problem," Wyn said with a shrug.

"Just for you. Not for him," I said, locking eyes with Mr. Baker so he knew exactly how I felt.

"Oh! And before you go . . ." Mr. Wyatt picked up one of the folded maps Wyn had discovered earlier, then he scooted his chair across the floor to reach a nearby file cabinet. He pulled out a manila folder and gently placed the folded map inside. "I gave Tig a souvenir, and you should get to have one, too."

He winked at Wyn warmly, then theater-whispered loudly enough for the whole room to hear. "Just in case Mr. Baker doesn't let you back upstairs." I slipped the folder and the hollowed-out book into my backpack and zipped it tight.

Mr. Baker huffed in irritation and looked at his watch. "Quickly, girls, some of us have other things to do," he snapped.

Wyn and I strode across the room and out the library door. Mr. Baker shut the door crisply behind us, then immediately began loping down the stairs at a swift pace.

"I don't know what he told you, but forget about it. There are some things that simply don't concern you. Things that should be left to the adults. Those who respect the history of this town," Mr. Baker snapped over his shoulder. "Doddering old fool. Never satisfied, even after all the meddling he's done."

He quickly outpaced us and disappeared around the corner of a hallway, leaving Wyn and me to more leisurely make our way back to the auditorium.

"God, that guy is the worst!" I said loudly, hoping he'd hear.

"'Things that should be left to the adults,'" Wyn said mockingly. "Whatever. He certainly didn't complain when we rescued him and his friends from getting picked off like fish in a barrel."

"That's for sure," I agreed. "And what was all that about Mr. Wyatt meddling? Do you think that was about The Hunt?"

"I mean, maybe?" Wyn said. "I honestly thought he was exaggerating about all the drama and deaths and whatever, but maybe some of the Murder of Crows people actually care about this treasure hunt. I vote we grab some cake, hear the rest of what Mr. Wyatt has to tell us, and then get the hell out of here."

"Agreed."

We rounded the corner of the last stairwell and headed back down into the foyer by the door.

Roughly half the guests had returned to the auditorium for cake, and right near the front of the line was the woman with the severe haircut who had met us at the door.

When we first saw her, she had been pinched with disapproval, and she had a similar expression now. (Who's mad when they're eating cake?) When she caught sight of us, the woman looked over our shoulders, toward the staircase, and her eyes seemed to darken in realization.

We watched as she grabbed three tiny plates of cake from the table and made her way toward us.

"Excuse me, I don't believe we've had the honor of meeting. I'm Noel." She inclined her head toward us, a handshake currently out of the question.

Noel handed me and Wyn the small paper plates. It was obvious she'd just grabbed the extra cake to use as a conversation starter. I decided not to call her out on it.

"Tig, I was wondering if I might have a moment alone. Perhaps your friend could take a piece of cake up to Mr. Wyatt while we chat." Noel phrased the question more like a command, and she handed the third piece of cake to Wyn without waiting for an answer.

"I was already planning to do that," Wyn scoffed, taking the plate. "I'll be back, Tig."

Noel watched as Wyn sashayed from the room, then turned to me and placed her own slice of cake onto the table behind her.

"Your speech was very good. I wanted to let you know how much I appreciate the work you did on the Lit Killer case. I knew Harry Levinson personally—as we all did—and it was such a disappointment to learn how pathetic he actually was. For how smart he thought he was, it never once occurred to him to appropriately manage his dysfunctions with therapy. What a messy and selfish way to deal with his problems."

"You could put it that way, I guess," I said, glancing around to see if anyone was listening to our conversation.

"I can, and I did," Noel said with a small smirk. "I heard from Mr. Green that you turned down the membership offer.

That's disappointing, since it is your birthright, you know," she said mysteriously. "Although perhaps Mr. Wyatt filled you in?"

I narrowed my eyes suspiciously. This conversation sure wasn't going the way I expected it to.

To my surprise, she threw her head back and laughed with glee. "And there's the famous Torres grit!" Noel said, snapping her finger sharply. "You're so much like your aunt. But even more like your grandmother, I think. Now *she* was a sharpshooter with attitude. Strong women—gotta love them."

"You knew Abuela and my aunt?" I perked up.

Noel waved her hand in a so-so motion and shrugged. "Your aunt only in passing around town. She tended to steer clear of me on Sofia's orders. For all I adored her, your grandmother can hold a grudge longer than a fish can hold its breath."

That was too confusing to merit a real response. "Okay," I replied blandly. "Can we go back to the birthright part?"

But Noel was no longer looking at me. Over my shoulder, she was watching Wyn make her way from the stairs back toward the auditorium, the plate still in her hands. Noel could tell her time with me was dwindling to a close.

"I'd recommend asking your grandmother about that—see what she has to say," she said quickly. Noel reached into her purse and removed her wallet and a pen. She took out a business card, scribbled something on the back, and then handed it to me.

"If you're free, I would love to invite you and Sofia over for tea one day. Anytime will do. She'll . . . Well. She'll tell you that we had some difficulties in the past, but please let her know that I'd love to catch up. I miss her. Dearly."

I reached out to accept the card, and just as my fingertips touched the paper, there was a shrill scream from the back of the room. I turned around just in time to see Mr. Wyatt sailing down from his cutout window headfirst. His body was unmoving and stiff, his limbs stuck out this way and that, not doing anything to stop the pull of gravity on his frail form. For a second, my mind flashed back to Tony Del Canto falling from the library tower, and I fought a wave of nausea.

Mr. Wyatt finally landed, quite unfortunately, directly on top of the cake with a monstrous crash. Icing mixed with blood flew in all directions, slapping wetly against the walls, furniture, and guests, a thick smear coating the side of my face. There was a moment of silence; then the screaming began. Some of the members immediately ran for the door, but Noel, Mr. Green, Mayor Highsmith, and I darted forward toward the body.

"Alan!" Mr. Green cried. He knelt by the body and felt for a pulse.

"Well, if the fall didn't kill him, something certainly did. He fell like a brick," Mayor Highsmith said bluntly.

I reached out to check his pulse myself. There was nothing there, and his skin was strangely heated and clammy. I rubbed my hand on the side of my pants.

"TIG!" Wyn pushed her way through the pandemonium. "What happened? I heard a scream."

But she immediately slipped on the icing as she got closer to the body—still in her stocking feet—and with a screech, she careened into Noel from behind. The plate of cake still in Wyn's hand slipped from her grip in the collision and slammed against the wall behind them.

"Get off me!" Noel shouted, her voice high in shock and panic. Her eyes were wild.

Wyn steadied herself against me and blinked slowly. "I was just going up to see him. I didn't even make it all the way up the stairs. I forgot a fork . . ." She trailed off. "Is . . . is he dead?"

But before anyone could answer, the table legs—loaded down by cake and having taken the brunt of Mr. Wyatt's fall—suddenly gave out with a resounding crash. Mr. Wyatt's body rolled from the table to the floor, and the back of his skull fell off with a wet clatter.

The mayor heaved. Noel covered her eyes and let out a hysterical moan of anguish.

"Noel, go call the police," Mr. Green said firmly.

He brushed his fingers tenderly against Mr. Wyatt's face and took a deep breath. "My dear, you didn't deserve this."

Then he looked up at me and Wyn, still gaping down at the corpse, filthy with icing and smeared with blood.

"I think it's time you two saw your way home."

I thought the Lit Killer was done, and so was this podcast. But a suspicious death happening at the club full of people Levinson had been hunting, right after I showed up to talk about Levinson? Maybe my podcast is saying that it's not done with me.

It didn't slip my mind at all that Mr. Wyatt had been giving us forbidden information right before he died. Places like Hollow Falls . . . your past always comes back to haunt you. I knew that better than anyone—and I guess so did Mr. Wyatt. The book and spyglass he'd given me burned a hole in my backpack all the way home.

Of course the way he'd died was suspicious. People don't just careen out of windows for fun. He could barely get from one end of his office to the other without a walker. It was unlikely he had managed to propel himself out the window with enough force to land where he did—and certainly not accidentally.

No, if you asked me, it looked like someone had either pushed him really hard, or they used his spectacular fall as a distraction to accomplish something else. After all, Mr. Green did say his house was full of secrets. And there's nothing more distracting than watching your host fall to his death while being showered in blood and sugar.

I wish I had gotten a chance to see who was downstairs right before it all happened. Noel cornered me, and then there was too much going on to really be able to tell. It's hard to find a suspect in chaos like that.

The only person I knew for a fact wasn't down there was Wyn. And judging by the sweat on her forehead and the cake in her clutches, she hadn't made it far before she'd turned around and come back down. So not only did she not make it up to the library in time to witness his death, but she also missed when everyone started rushing around in a panic. And that stairwell was so dark, the killer could have been right there and she might not have even noticed.

There goes my hope for a smooth murder-less transition into the new school year.

But maybe not. Perhaps the trauma of the

last year had me seeing murder where there wasn't any. Mr. Wyatt's death *could* have been an accident–he was ancient. Maybe it was just an old man losing his balance near an open window? Or he could have had a heart attack or a stroke or an aneurysm. Or any of those other medical conditions that will kill a feeble old man before his body hits the ground.

But I still couldn't shake how nervous he seemed when he'd spoken to us in the library. And how he had hidden that spyglass and asked me to keep it safe. Not to mention all that talk of factions in the MOC still being involved in The Hunt . . .

God, I wish he had gotten to finish telling us the rest of what he knew—and how Wyn, Max, and I were supposed to find some dead founder who'd been missing for over a century.

The book he'd hidden the spyglass in was a good place to start, though. And it made for interesting bus reading on the way home. It spoke of a long history of deaths, both explained and unexplained, but many of them violent and linked to a mysterious treasure:

The Hunt. But as there was a giant hole in the center of the book, I quickly hit a dead end.

I couldn't shake it. There was just something so sinister about Mr. Wyatt dying right after he asked us to help him. And I didn't feel right letting him down.

His dying wish was for me to protect this spyglass and learn more about The Hunt. To find his treasure before anyone else lost their lives to it. And I had already failed.

Now I had an even bigger mission: to figure out who was responsible for Mr. Wyatt's death and to make sure they never got their hands on that treasure.

Chapter 7

The light in our kitchen was still visible from the street when I got off the bus, even though it was almost eleven and Abuela rarely stays up late. Dad liked to be up all hours of the night when he was in between stints on the oil tanker. But ever since he left a few weeks ago, it had been really quiet in our house.

When I entered the front door, I spotted a half-full cup of tea on the coffee table in the living room and an open book next to it.

"I'm home!" I called as I made my way into the kitchen. "Why are you still awake?"

"Welcome!" Abuela said. She was cutting apples by the sink. A box of gingersnap cookies was on the counter next to her. "I got sucked into a book, and by the time I looked up, it was late and I was hungry again. How was your party?"

I pulled out a chair and sat down at the kitchen table.

"Uh, it wasn't quite a party. The Murder of Crows invited me to do a speech about the Lit Killer case . . . and then someone died."

"Someone died?!" Abuela whirled around and then paused. "Why are you covered in icing?"

"Uh, Mr. Wyatt? The guy who hosts the meetings? He fell from his balcony onto the refreshment table. Hence . . ." I gestured down to my buttercream-covered clothes.

"I talked to him before he died," I said softly. "He said he knew you."

"Oh," Abuela said, in a tone I hadn't heard her use before. Curious but careful. Much less panicked than she'd been before my explanation but significantly less panicked than I thought she'd be, considering I just told her I saw yet another person plummet to their death.

Abuela turned around and resumed cutting, this time a bit slower than before. I hadn't exactly told Abuela where I was heading before I left earlier in the night. Things had been difficult after Mr. Levinson was brought to justice. The resolution of that case had scared her more than I thought it would. It wasn't that Abuela didn't let me talk about what happened.

It was more that, whenever I mentioned it, the room would fill with such sharp melancholy that eventually I'd stopped bringing it up altogether. It didn't seem worth getting her upset over a Q&A with the Murder of Crows about stuff that had already happened.

However, seeing the uncharacteristic tension in Abuela's shoulders, I was beginning to regret that strategy.

"I'm sorry I didn't tell you earlier. It wasn't, like, a planned thing. I had run into this Mr. Green guy at the bus stop this afternoon, and he gave me an invitation. The Murder of Crows were really impacted by what happened with Mr. Levinson, obviously. I think they really just wanted closure from the whole ordeal. Wyn came with me and helped with the presentation."

"What did you think of Alan?" she asked quietly.

My ears perked up. I half expected Abuela to deny knowing any of the MOC members or totally change the subject. This was intriguing.

"Tall, old, really nice," I finally replied. "He wanted to give me a gift for all I had done. And Wyn and I got to ask him a few questions for an article we're writing for the school paper." Okay, that last bit was bending the truth a little. But I wanted to see how much I could get out of Abuela before revealing my hand.

"I know I only knew him for, like, a half hour, but he didn't seem like the kind of person who deserved to go out like that. It was terrible."

Abuela flinched, her shoulders tightening.

I dug the book out of my bag, leaving the spyglass still inside, and placed it on the table. Abuela turned around and walked to the table to look at it, an inscrutable expression on her warm face. She stroked the spine of the book and ran her hand across the gilded pages, examining it under the fluorescent kitchen light. I could tell that she recognized it—but I couldn't tell if she knew what was inside.

"I knew him a long time ago. When I was young," Abuela murmured. "He must have really liked you; he doesn't give away pieces of his library to just anyone."

Abuela paused, her fingers still lingering against the old book. "Did you meet anyone else?" Abuela asked the question casually, but I knew it was loaded. She was trying to find out what I knew, just like I was doing to her.

"I . . . uh . . . I also met a guy named Judah who wants to interview me or something," I said. Noel's card was burning a hole in my pocket.

"Judah is very nice!" Abuela said. She sounded grateful for the subject change. "Very smart! I remember he did a speech on Founder's Day back when he was in elementary school.

He's probably a few years older than you, but he's a good boy. You should have him on your podcast."

"Yeah," I said, coughing lightly. I fingered Noel's card for a bit before slowly placing it on the table. "I also met a woman named Noel."

Abuela's face went from encouraging to blank so fast, it sent a shiver up my spine.

"Did she talk to you?" she demanded.

"She did, but not for very long. We got interrupted by—well. By Mr. Wyatt. But before that, she said all this vague stuff about you, and she asked if you'd be interested in coming over for tea at her—"

"No." Abuela cut me off so vehemently that I jerked back in surprise.

"What? Why? What's the deal between you guys?" I asked.

Instead of answering, Abuela turned around, picked up the plate of gingersnaps and apple slices, and left the room. I looked down at the card lying untouched on the table and picked it up. I turned it over and read what Noel had scribbled on the back. I remembered her words about grudges and the way her eyebrows had crinkled with despair when offering the invitation.

I followed Abuela into the living room.

"I need a minute to process this whole thing. Don't bother me about this again, Tig," she said, her tone sharp with warning. Her book was in her hand and her reading glasses were on, but I could tell she wasn't reading.

"Noel seemed sad, or at least like she had some regrets. She gave me this card for you." I held out the card, but Abuela didn't take it. She shifted so the card was pointing at her shoulder and turned the page of her book. I had never seen her act this way in my entire life. It was shockingly petty.

I relented and put the card back into my pocket.

"If you don't want to tell me what's going on, fine," I said stubbornly. "But I'm going to talk to her. She said it was my birthright. Whatever 'it' means, I was hoping *you* would be the one to tell me—not her."

Abuela slammed her book shut and stood up.

"There are some things that I cannot speak about," she began quietly. "There are some people that I will not see again. I am not strong enough for it. Please respect that."

Abuela picked the plate up from the coffee table and tucked her book under her arm. When she turned to me again, her face looked tired and much older, as if the effort to control her anger had reduced her somehow. "Good night, mija. I'll see you in the morning."

The encounter left me feeling strange and a bit dizzy as I

stood in the living room, rooted to the floor, staring at the space Abuela had abruptly vacated.

I lay on my bed in the dark, flipping Noel's card back and forth in my hands. The room was awash in the blue of moonlight, and the tick of my wall clock seemed loud in the silence. I glanced over at my podcast recording equipment, then back at the card.

At dawn and dusk: even so, Noel had written.

I picked up my phone off the nightstand and unplugged it from the charger. It felt like snooping, but my curiosity and irritation were higher than my consideration at the moment. I typed the words from the card into Google and pressed search.

It was . . . from a poem?

I squinted at the tiny letters on the screen:

"Even So" by Victor James Daley

The days go by—the days go by,
Sadly and wearily to die:
    Each with its burden of small cares,

Each with its sad gift of gray hairs
For those who sit, like me, and sigh,
"The days go by! The days go by!"
Ah, nevermore on shining plumes,
Shedding a rain of rare perfumes
That men call memories, they are borne
As in life's many-visioned morn,
When Love sang in the myrtle-blooms—
Ah, nevermore on shining plumes!

Where is my life? Where is my life?
The morning of my youth was rife
With promise of a golden day.
Where have my hopes gone? Where are they—
The passion and the splendid strife?
Where is my life? Where is my life?

My thoughts take hue from this wild day,
And, like the skies, are ashen gray;
The sharp rain, falling constantly,
Lashes with whips of steel the sea:
What words are left for Hope to say?
My thoughts take hue from this wild day.

I dreamt—my life is all a dream!—
That I should sing a song supreme
  To gladden all sad eyes that weep,
  And take the Harp to Time, and sweep
Its chords to some eternal theme.
I dreamt—my life is all a dream.

The world is very old and wan—
The sun that once so brightly shone
  Is now as pale as the pale moon.
  I would that Death came swift and soon;
For all my dreams are dead and gone.
The world is very old and wan.

The world is young, the world is strong,
But I in dreams have wandered long.
  God lives. What can Death do to me
  The sun is shining on the sea.
Yet shall I sing my splendid song—
The world is young, the world is strong.

Well. That was intense. Noel was around Abuela's age—maybe she was sick and trying to tie up loose ends before it was too late? Knowing the secret message she had intended to send to Abuela was potentially news of her fading away, while also knowing Abuela would never receive it, was actually pretty uncomfortable.

I got up and crept out of my room and down the hallway. It was nearly midnight, and the entire house was silent. Abuela was probably sleeping already. I tiptoed to a stop in front of her door and placed the card, note-side up, directly in front of it. Abuela would be furious. But she would have to bend down to see what it was first and she couldn't do that without unintentionally reading what Noel had written for her.

They had both already lost one friend today. Maybe this could help them from losing another.

The next morning, the house was quiet and still. Normally on a Saturday I would wake up to Abuela grilling tostadas and the smell of café con leche, while the sounds of trova filled the house with life. But today there was just the sound of birds and the cars outside.

Abuela must really be angry.

I got up and headed for the kitchen. As I passed through the main hallway, I saw that the space in front of Abuela's bedroom door where I had left Noel's card was clear. My heart sank.

I knocked on the door and waited for an answer, but there was none. I gently pushed inside, but she wasn't there.

In the kitchen, placed neatly on the table, was the shiny foil of a Pop-Tart packet, lovingly arranged, a note, and Noel's card.

Went to the park and then grocery shopping. I'll see you later this afternoon. I love you very much. Sorry. Abuela

I picked up Noel's card. In Abuela's neat spindly handwriting, right underneath Noel's loopy scrawl, were two words written in bright red pen: "Sonnet 34."

Guiltily, I took out my phone and googled it.

Sonnet 34 by William Shakespeare

Why didst thou promise such a beauteous day,
And make me travel forth without my cloak,
To let base clouds o'ertake me in my way,
Hiding thy bravery in their rotten smoke?
'Tis not enough that through the cloud thou break,
To dry the rain on my storm-beaten face,
For no man well of such a salve can speak
That heals the wound and cures not the disgrace:
Nor can thy shame give physic to my grief;
Though thou repent, yet I have still the loss:
The offender's sorrow lends but weak relief

To him that bears the strong offence's cross.
Ah! but those tears are pearl which thy love sheds,
And they are rich and ransom all ill deeds.

Harsh. Whatever Noel did must have been brutal. Well, at least Abuela didn't seem to be upset at me anymore. I guess this was just one more thing to toss in the Trauma Closet and lock the door.

Noel, on the other hand? She was fair game. Like it or not, she was going to help me get to the bottom of Abuela's involvement in The Hunt and her history with the Murder of Crows—and how it was all connected to Mr. Wyatt's death.

But first, I needed to talk to my friends.

Chapter 8

Promptly at noon, Wyn, Max, and Ella crashed into the *Talon* office and made their way to the desk where I was working at the computer. Wyn looked almost manic with energy.

"Hey, Tig!" She waved.

Ella, beside her was scowling. "I don't know why I had to be here. I told you guys I don't want anything to do with this Murder of Crows nonsense. And no one is spilling any good tea for my column *here*," she griped.

I didn't say it out loud, but she was kind of right. It also made me feel weird to think about Wyn contacting Ella without me, but I didn't know why. I guess it could have something to do with Ella being Tormentor #1 when I'd come back to Hollow Falls last year, but we'd both moved on from that. It was almost like . . . jealousy?

I shook my head quickly in an attempt to refocus. I did not need these confusing feelings on top of everything else that had happened in the last twenty-four hours.

This morning, even though Abuela wasn't in the kitchen making breakfast, I could still feel her anger and hurt in the bones of the house.

I had dialed and deleted my dad's number six times but never pressed call. I wanted to call him—both to see if he knew anything else about Abuela's history with the MOC and to tell him I was wrapped up in yet another violent death. It made sense to call him. But what could he do out on an oil tanker in the middle of the ocean besides worry?

"How are you doing?" Wyn asked me. "I missed the main event, and I still had nightmares about a cake that leaked blood." She shuddered.

"Eh, I'm fine. Kind of used to seeing death up close and personal at this point." I shrugged, feigning nonchalance. Wyn and Max had their own nightmares from all we'd been through. They didn't need to hear about mine, too.

"But I'm glad you guys are here!" I said, quick to change the subject. "I have some theories about everything that happened yesterday—and how it's all connected to The Hunt."

"Speaking of!" Max interrupted. "I know you all think Founder's Day is just a cutesy small-town tradition that no one cares about—and TBH, you're not totally wrong. But I just think that coming at the piece from the angle of the celebration's violent origin story is maybe not the move. Historic deaths—be they murder or accidental—is not really the vibe we should be going for when people are coming back to school with Levinson still on the brain.

"And sure, this whole situation is mysterious—and it sucks that that old dude died right after your presentation, yikes—but a puff piece will take half the time as a true investigation and will make people happier, and I *know* you know that, Wyn."

Somehow hearing them bicker began to relax me a bit. It felt so normal and trivial that I almost wanted to laugh.

"I get where you're coming from, Max. But if anyone cares about my opinion as one quarter of the *Talon*'s staff"—Ella looked at us pointedly—"I think we should follow this rabbit hole about Mr. Wyatt and The Hunt. A man falling dead into a cake isn't really a story one can ignore."

Max looked really frustrated. "No one's really gotten a chance to get over what happened last spring. If we do a story about the town history and the meaning of community, maybe it will help people figure out a way to process this stuff," he explained. "If we do a story on the Wyatt cake murder or whatever, I think it will honestly just scare people."

"I think at this point we can all agree that people deserve to be scared." I laughed dryly. "But it's not just Mr. Wyatt's death. I think this all points to something bigger—something that's been going on for a long time."

I paused for dramatic effect—hosting a podcast had at least taught me that much.

"Wyn, you know that rude woman Noel who cornered me downstairs before the cake hit the fan? While you were gone, she mentioned knowing Abuela, but she was super cagey about how she knew her and why they fell out. That, combined with what Mr. Wyatt said upstairs about knowing Abuela, too, well, it got me feeling curious.

"Noel gave me this card and asked me to give it to Abuela." I dug Noel's card out of my pocket and handed it to Max so the others could get a look at it. He flipped it around in his hand and held it up. Ella peered in close, then clicked her tongue.

"This is premium card stock. It doesn't even bend at all." Ella seemed impressed. "What does this stuff on the back mean? 'At dawn and dusk, even so'? Sonnet 34? What does this have to do with The Hunt?"

"I actually don't know yet," I admitted, settling back into

my chair. "But Noel got all mad that I turned down Mr. Green's offer to join the Murder of Crows because it was my 'birthright' or something. And then she mentioned something about Abuela having 'Torres grit' and told me to ask Abuela what she was talking about."

"Your grandma is, like . . . the mildest lady in the whole town—no offense," Wyn said.

"Yeah, that's what I thought, too!" I exclaimed in frustration. "That is until I went home and tried to tell Abuela about meeting Mr. Wyatt and how Noel asked us over for tea, and Abuela started acting all suspicious and refused to go. She even yelled at me for asking her what was going on."

"What did she say this morning?" Ella asked, putting her purse on the ground and then sliding into a nearby chair. For not caring about this "Murder of Crows nonsense," Ella seemed invested.

"Nothing." I shook my head. "When I woke up, she was gone. She had left me a note apologizing, which was nice, but it was very clear that she did not want to talk about it anymore."

"So, it looks like we're stumbling upon some spooky secrets?" Wyn said, raising an eyebrow.

"More like painful secrets. Anyway, she reacted so dramatically, I got curious and looked up the stuff written on the back. The black pen is Noel's and the red is what Abuela wrote on it this morning before she completely ghosted me. They're both poems. I think Abuela wanted me to give the card back to Noel." I paused. "Abuela's poem was . . . mean."

Max pulled out his phone and looked up "Even So" and read it out loud while Wyn and Ella listened closely.

As Max got to the parts of the poem with death, he began glancing at me, Wyn, and Ella with increasing concern. Ella was listening keenly and nodding along to a few of the lines, as if she was thinking about it just as hard as I had.

"What's Abuela's poem about?" she asked when Max finished.

"Uh . . . it's Shakespeare. It's about betrayal, I think. It's also weirdly passionate? I don't even know how to feel about it, but I'm definitely not going to bring that up in person."

Max returned to Google and looked up Sonnet 34. Before he began to read this one out loud, he paused and scanned it quickly.

"Yikes," Max said, bringing to life exactly what Abuela thought about Noel's apology poem.

"'Nor can thy shame give physic to my grief'? 'Though thou repent, yet I have still the loss'?" He was reading the lines out in an extra-offended voice, like they were lyrics on a diss track. "What the hell did this woman do to your grandma?"

"I wish I knew," I said dubiously. "But I don't think it's all a coincidence. I think my abuela had something to do with The Hunt. And I have to get her to tell me what she knows so that we can find the founder's body and the treasure."

"WHAT?" three voices blared at me in surround sound.

"Guys, hear me out! Mr. Wyatt's *dying wish* was for us to help him find the treasure and put an end to the violence. We couldn't save him, but we can stop anyone else from getting hurt in pursuit of this weird old local legend. We can't go back on what we promised—not after what happened."

My friends continued to stare at me silently, their expressions ranging from shock (Max) to disbelief (Wyn) to doubt (Ella).

"Plus," I started again, "we're going to get a killer front-page story out of it—pun intended—and maybe even the next season of my podcast."

"Podcast?" Wyn finally said, surprised. "Whoa, whoa, whoa. I thought you were done with that. Since we caught the Lit Killer and all."

I shook my head. "I wasn't planning on continuing now that Levinson is locked up. He was my mission, you know? But I'm starting to think the overarching story of the 'mystery and history' of Hollow Falls isn't over yet. Something about The Hunt and what we've stumbled onto here feels like . . .

when you pull a thread and your whole sweater starts unraveling."

"Is there any way we can talk you out of this?" Max asked, already knowing the answer.

I shook my head and grinned.

"Fine." He sighed, pulling out a chair to sit down next to me. "Then I'm sure as hell not going to let you do it alone. Where do we start? The Hunt, right? That seems to be where this all started. If people were really that mad about Mr. Wyatt burying it all those years ago, maybe one of them finally came back for revenge?"

"That's what I'm thinking, too. And The Hunt is actually why I asked you to meet me here," I said, gesturing to the underwhelming *Talon* offices.

"Ella, you remember how you said that they destroyed all the original riddles for The Hunt back in the '70s?"

Ella nodded slowly, not sure where this was going.

"Well, I was thinking . . . what if they missed a couple?" My friends stared at me blankly, and I plowed ahead. "Mr. Wyatt and the city purged the public records of books and old newspapers about the riddles fifty years ago, right? But they probably didn't think to check the *Talon*. It's a school newspaper; it's not the *New York Times* . . . or even the *Hollow Falls Ledger*. We all know people don't really consider us a source of news. So, maybe a few of those lost riddles have slipped through the cracks."

"Oh my god, the archives!" Wyn shouted, catching on. "Every issue of the *Talon* since the paper started in the 1950s is available on the Hollow Falls High intranet. They digitized and uploaded PDFs of everything a few years ago. I helped with the tail end of it when Judah blocked me from writing anything." Wyn rolled her eyes.

"So we can look through them by year and search key words within each year to read old articles?" Max asked. "And maybe find the missing riddles?"

"Exactly." I grinned. "And now might be a good time to mention I got here a little early and I already found them."

"WHAT?" Max and Wyn exclaimed in unison.

"Way to bury the lede," Ella said with a smile. She looked impressed in spite of herself.

"Yeah, they published a copy in the *Talon* back in 1956. Someone did a refresher story for Easter calling the founder's treasure the greatest Easter egg hunt or whatever. It's absolutely just a puff piece, but the riddles' distribution was commonly accessible then, so there wasn't a reason for them not to publish them in full in the school paper," I explained. "They didn't really go into detail about how they work, but I'm sure we can figure it out."

I pulled up the tab with the article in question on my computer and read the riddles out loud.

"Number one: 'Daniel is yet the father of this babe. Heaven.'

"Number two: 'What makes a monster and what makes a man? Hell.'

"Number three: 'Treason and patriotism; wait and hope; time and silence. Hell.'

"Number four: 'A dark night with bright stars. Heaven.'

"Number five: 'A great and terrible adventure of tradition and absurdity. Earth.'

"Number six: 'The eternal probable improbability, both divine and worldly, blood and bone over soil. Heaven.'"

Wyn had begun typing wildly.

"No way, no way, no way," she was mumbling.

"What?" Max asked, whipping around to face her screen.

"Ha!" Wyn pressed enter and then sat back from her monitor triumphantly. "You know when you learn about Founder's Day in elementary school and they show you that old map of the town? I think that map shows the locations given by the first two riddles."

On Wyn's screen was a scan of a map of Hollow Falls. Two locations were marked with thick black Xs, with some text typed neatly beside them.

"This is the earliest map in the archive, and they gave it out to third graders, so I'm sure it's incomplete, but it's a start!" Wyn said. She expanded the map so it took up the whole screen and zoomed in so we could read the clues.

The riddles here looked longer than the ones from the article from the 1950s. Next to the map's tiny church it said "Daniel is yet the father of this babe. Heaven." But below that, there was something else: *The Scarlet Letter.*

I shuddered involuntarily. When I first came back to Hollow Falls and was digging through Aunt Beth's stuff, the very first clue I found was connected to the same book. What new rabbit hole was I about to drag everybody down into?

And then my detective brain took over. "This map shows us how to figure out the answers. The riddles point to a book—and then the clue and the book together must point you to a place in town!"

"But not all of these buildings are right," Ella said, leaning in close to the monitor to get a better look. "Look, there's the town square, and that old fountain, which means this building should be the coffee shop, not the founder's house, and this one should be that fancy Italian place, not the train depot."

"You're right," I said, deflating a little.

"But wouldn't we need an older map anyway?" Max asked. "Like, Old Man Hollow was obviously not picking up a cold brew on his way to the mines in the nineteenth century."

Suddenly, things began clicking together. "Max, you're a genius!" I said, smacking a kiss on his cheek. "Wyn, do you remember that map Mr. Wyatt gave you?"

Her eyes lit up, and she raced to grab my backpack from the other side of the room. She dug inside and pulled out the fragile, yellowing paper. When she spread it over the large desk in the front of the room, we all gasped.

This map was much older than the one from the archives. It was labeled "1858"—just a few years after the town was founded. Wyn pointed to the border of the map where tight writing in pencil filled up the blank space. "Look!"

"That's Abuela's handwriting!" I exclaimed. "She was filling in the answers! Or . . . at least some of them. I *knew* she had something to do with all of this." I took out my phone and snapped a few pictures of the map and a close-up image of the riddles.

"But what about the heaven-hell-or-earth thing? How does that come into play?" Max asked.

"I don't know," I said. "Maybe it's some play on good and evil? Or what you might be looking for specifically? But I know someone we can ask."

I walked back to the computer and huffed into my chair, rolling a little. "I just wish I knew why Abuela shut down on me last night. What happened fifty years ago?"

I turned back to my computer. "Before I found the riddles, I'd been searching the names of people in the Murder of Crows and key words like 'riddle' and 'treasure.' It's bonkers how mainstream this was before the knowledge was purged. It's not like something shady she needs to keep hidden from me.

"People even talked pretty casually about the deaths of participants in The Hunt throughout the years. It seems like the violence had been dying down, but it escalated sharply right around when Abuela would have been looking."

"Too bad we can't talk to Mr. Wyatt more," Ella said. She had perched back in front of her computer, too, and was scrolling aimlessly. "It looks like he was really in the thick of things back then." She turned her screen so we could see. She had a scan of the 1954 yearbook up.

"Oh my *god*. He was hot," Max said shamelessly.

He wasn't wrong. Teenage Alan Wyatt had his hair greased back like a gangster and looked way too menacing for an eighteen-year-old, but there he was in black and white.

"There's a picture of Mr. Wyatt and Mr. Green in the 1961 yearbook, too. Apparently Mr. Wyatt taught here for a while and sponsored Mr. Green's sporting club after school."

Ella pulled up another tab, pushing the monitor over so Max, Wyn, and I could see. It was an image of Mr. Wyatt and Mr. Green looking painfully young, dressed in old fencing clothes. Their net masks were in their hands. Mr. Green's face was open and bright as he smiled for the camera, but Mr. Wyatt still looked stern, his rapier loosely gripped in his hand while Mr. Green's was lying on the floor.

"It's eerie seeing them so young like that . . ." Wyn said. It was clear we were all thinking it.

"It reminds me of us a bit. Just a little older," I admitted.

"Hey, Tig," Max said cautiously. "I think I found something about your grandma."

We all scrambled to meet Max behind his computer.

"It's an article about one of those Hunt deaths that happened at the church. 'Man Falls from Church Balcony, The Hunt Claims Another Life.'"

I skimmed the article, scrolling fast.

"It says that Abuela and Noel were interviewed—they were the last people to see him alive. This must have been the death Mr. Wyatt was talking about. The one that made them decide to shut The Hunt down. And maybe it's why Noel and Abuela don't talk anymore."

My brain was racing a million miles a minute. I needed to talk to Abuela or check out the locations on the map or *something*.

"Hey, take a breath," Wyn said, placing a hand on my arm. I hadn't even realized I'd started pacing.

"We have to go back to the scene of the crime. We don't have enough information. This started with Mr. Wyatt's death. Maybe there is something in his library that will offer us a clue as to why—after years of no activity—this is all picking up again."

"Don't look at me," Ella said. "I'm not breaking into a dead man's house. I wouldn't even break into an alive man's house."

I could feel Max and Wyn looking at her judgmentally and almost let out a huff of laughter.

"Well, I can," Wyn said. "Does nine tonight work for you?"

Max sighed. "I *guess* it does."

"Okay. Good." I nodded, flopping back into the closest chair. "I'm really glad that I can count on you guys.

"Let's go get some answers."

Chapter 9

"You know, when I was a kid, I genuinely didn't think this was the kind of criminal I would become. I always thought I would choose something glamorous like tax evasion or art theft," Max said blithely as he swung his leg over the police tape. "Not busting into dead people's houses."

"I like how you were pretty sure you'd become a criminal in the first place." I snorted, opting instead to duck beneath the tape.

"Really? You couldn't see me as, like . . . a debonair gentleman thief?" Max was heading toward the front door of Mr. Wyatt's house.

"Dude, the front door is not gonna be open. We should be trying windows," Wyn hissed into the night behind him.

Max rolled his eyes but trudged back to the side of the house to start tugging on window handles. After twenty minutes of trying, one of the windows in the basement budged, and we were able to pry it up. I shimmied in first, landing on a large wooden dining room table that had been crammed in the back of the basement with a bunch of other furniture. I helped Wyn and Max down into the darkness.

"I'm going to turn on my recorder. You never know what we could stumble upon in the dark," I said.

"I'm personally hoping we find silence," Max said.

I glared at him.

"But . . . that's just me," he finished.

Wyn turned her phone flashlight on and lit the way up the stairs and to the basement door, each step echoing loudly through the empty house.

"You have got to be quiet!" Max hissed.

"Why would we need to be quiet?" Wyn asked.

"This is still a crime scene," I pointed out. "We're not supposed to be here. What if one of the neighbors hears noise or sees movement? I don't want to have to deal with the cops and explain to my abuela why we're here."

My abuela, who had run errands all day to ensure I couldn't ask her any follow-up questions about Noel and the poems and The Hunt.

The house was completely silent as we crept across the

wooden floors. Wyn angled her phone light away from the windows so people from the street couldn't see us poking around inside.

Police tape sealed off the auditorium and the staircase, but we ducked underneath it and went upstairs anyway. The house creaked, settling in the night, and Max jumped. Wyn snickered, and Max pushed her softly with a huff of annoyance.

The closer we got to the third floor, the creepier it felt to be in Mr. Wyatt's house. We didn't even know what we were looking for—and a man had *just* died here.

But my heart sped up as we approached the yawning darkness of the library. The door was open ahead of us, and for the first time since walking into the house, I heard purposeful noise. It sounded like it was coming from Mr. Wyatt's attached office.

I pulled the library door open wider, and the three of us entered silently in single file. The room felt . . . different than it did last night, when Mr. Wyatt had first told us his reason for inviting us to the Murder of Crows. I thought it would feel like a tomb, considering what happened just moments later, but it felt . . . alive somehow.

I held my finger to my lips as we approached the secret entrance to the office. "There's someone in there," I told Max and Wyn quietly, pointing to where the bookshelf was slightly askew—the only hint at the hidden space that lay behind it.

We crept along the edge of the library, moving closer to Mr. Wyatt's office, where the sound of rustling papers was barely audible.

Max, who had gone to the left while Wyn and I had stayed right, made it to the door first. He silently picked up a rock displayed on one of the bookshelves and waited for me to open the door. I curled my free hand around the edge of the shelf and pulled it as slowly as I could to minimize the sound, until the space was wide enough for us to make our move.

There was a sharp gasp of breath as the intruder realized he wasn't alone. The figure was about as tall as Wyn and dressed in black from head to toe. He was wearing a plain black mask that only showed his eyes. He had a few pieces of paper in one hand, and the other was buried deep inside one of Mr. Wyatt's file cabinets. Books were strewn everywhere, all splayed open, their spines broken and ripped pages hanging loosely from their bindings.

"What are you doing?!" I shouted.

The man sprang into action. He scooped up the small pile of papers and books he'd accumulated on Mr. Wyatt's desk and, to my shock, turned to face the cutout window as if he was intending to jump—a macabre parallel to Mr. Wyatt's own death.

But Max was quicker. He lunged forward, snagging the back of the intruder's shirt, and the man let out a shriek as he was torn forcibly away from his escape.

He stumbled backward, slamming into Max, who wheezed in pain, but Max had enough wherewithal to push the intruder back again. The man, completely off balance and protecting the books in his arms, banged the side of his face hard against one of Mr. Wyatt's bookshelves. He lunged at the window again, but Max—who barely had enough room to stand in the tiny office—crouched down and grabbed his shirt from behind again.

Furious, he roared, "Get off me!" and swung a fist at Max, missing by a fraction of an inch. Seeing that his original plan wasn't going to work, he focused his attention on the only other exit. With precision, he took a step back, then rushed the doorway—right where I was standing. I could see the desperation in his eyes the moment our assailant faced me.

I froze, and before I could react, Wyn stepped in front of me and shoved me out of his path. It didn't faze him. The intruder drew back his arm and slammed Wyn brutally into the glass cabinet to her right, which shattered. Wyn screamed as glass rained down on her.

"Wyn!" Max and I shouted in unison. I lunged into the room to check on her. Max, his face white with rage, chased after the man, through the library and out into the hall, his feet thundering on the floor.

Wyn was breathing hard and shaking as she took off the light jean jacket she had worn for the cool, summer night air.

"Are you okay?" I said hysterically. "Are you hurt?"

"I don't know!" Wyn cried.

I brushed the glass from her hair as she ran her hands over her body, trying to shake the shards out of her clothes.

"Turn around," I said firmly.

There were a few pieces of glass that had cut right through her jacket and shirt, leaving long, bloody scrapes down her back. Her white T-shirt was rapidly soaking with blood. I pinched out a few of the pieces of glass that were stuck in her skin and tossed them to the floor.

"Is it bad?" she said, her voice trembling from shock.

"No, it probably hurts a lot and you're definitely bleeding, but nothing went too deep. God, that was so messed up!"

"I know!" Wyn laughed deliriously. "I can't believe that happened. I can't believe that even happened!"

I gave her my arm to lean on as she stepped gingerly out of the glass.

"Are you hurt anywhere else?" I asked, and Wyn shook her head.

Max burst back into the library, panting heavily, his face bright red from exertion and anger.

"He . . . got away," Max huffed, leaning over to rest his hands on his knees. "I could . . . barely see in the dark and . . . he jumped . . ."

Max paused for a moment to collect himself and made a square shape with his hands.

"He . . . jumped down . . . the dumbwaiter shaft," he said finally.

"What?! How?" I exclaimed.

"I have no idea, but he stuck his landing like a damn gymnast. I heard him keep running after he hit the ground," Max said morosely. "How's Wyn's back?"

"Wyn's okay. Just shaken and scratched," I informed him. "Did you see what the guy took?"

Max shook his head. "I don't think he found what he was looking for. He dropped the books in his arms as he ran, and they fell all over the place. He seemed pissed off, but not, like, mad that he dropped them. More like mad that he didn't find the one that he was looking for in the first place. He said, 'Where is it?' right before he jumped."

I took a long glance around the office and the connected library. Books were scattered everywhere, but none of the smaller drawers or the samples on the shelves seemed to have been touched. Which meant he had to have been looking for something large. One of the books maybe?

But if he was just looking for a book, why were they all lying open? Couldn't he have just looked at the covers or the spines and saved himself the trouble?

Unless . . .

"I know what he was after," I said. "He must have been looking for the book with the cutout. He wants the spyglass Mr. Wyatt gave us."

Max shook his head. "Okay, so Mr. Wyatt was right about people being bloodthirsty over this mess. Jeez. What have we gotten ourselves into?"

"I'm not totally sure, but we better figure it out fast."

Suddenly, Wyn swayed on her feet, and she reached out for our arms to steady herself.

"Do you mind if I go home with you?" Wyn asked. "I don't want my parents to see me like this."

"Yeah. Of course, Wyn," I said softly. "Anytime."

The spyglass would have to wait.

Wyn lay on my bed with her head buried in her arms, her blonde eyelashes spiked into wet points as she tried not to cry.

I tried to keep my eyes from the expanse of her stretched out before me as I pulled out smaller pieces of glass I couldn't get at earlier and dropped them into a dish nearby with a small clink.

Abuela had already gone to bed for the night by the time we got home. (I'd be impressed at her commitment to avoiding me if I wasn't so annoyed about it.) The house was very quiet, and it felt still in the dark of the night.

Wyn was taking the procedure in strained quiet, gasping whenever a piece tugged too hard against her skin on its way out. It was strange to see her so vulnerable like this. I had always imagined her as effortlessly tough. In the exact way that I knew that *I* was tough. But I was starting to understand that there were some things about Wyn that I had misunderstood.

I've never touched anybody like this before. I'd hugged people, held their hand, kissed them, and more . . . but I'd never had anyone lying still and tense, completely trusting, with their back to me, shirtless. As I dabbed at the lighter scratches with peroxide, Wyn hissed with pain.

"Sorry," I said gently.

"I can take it," Wyn mumbled, her eyes fluttering open, red and shiny.

"You shouldn't have to," I said. "I should have been in the front. I thought that Max could run in and stop the guy, but if he managed to get past Max, I could maybe hold the line and keep him from getting past me, too," I admitted, embarrassed. "But instead, I stood there like an idiot while you two took the hits."

Wyn huffed a soft laugh, and I could practically hear her rolling her eyes. "You don't need to be the hero of every situation, Tig. You're not the main character. None of us could have done anything better than what we did. We're lucky to be alive."

I pressed my lips together, still disappointed in myself, and didn't continue that line of thought.

"The bigger cuts are going to sting more, but after we disinfect them, I'll glue them shut so they won't open up again when you put on your shirt," I said.

"Glue them shut?!" Wyn said in alarm. She started to try to twist around, but I put a hand on her shoulder and pressed her back down.

"It's body glue!" I snatched it from my side and held it up so she could see the bottle.

Wyn visibly relaxed. "Every time I feel like I understand how things work, you radically shift my worldview. How is body glue even a thing?"

I thought for a minute, trying to remember. "I think it was used in the military first, but they just used superglue until something better was made."

Wyn grinned. "I love how you even knew the answer for that," she said in a soft, sleepy voice.

For some reason, my heart sped up. I daubed the last of her cuts with disinfectant and blew on them softly to take out the sting.

"I just read it somewhere."

Wyn nodded and closed her eyes again. "I know. You usually do."

I had finished bandaging all the smaller cuts and was nearly finished putting liquid bandage on the larger ones before either of us spoke again.

"So what's the plan for tomorrow?" Wyn asked suddenly. "I don't want to just sit at home. Not this time."

"Uh, I guess we could go to the Hollow Falls Library and do some more research—try to figure out those last few riddles? Maybe try to dig up a little more info on the founder?"

"Sounds good to me," Wyn answered with a sigh.

We sat in silence for another minute. "I'm glad you'll be there," I said softly. "It's not the same without you."

Wyn gazed at me from over her shoulder for a moment. She reached back, even though I could tell from her grimace that the gesture cost her, and squeezed my hand.

I rubbed the side of her thumb with mine, not wanting to let go.

I didn't sleep that night, I couldn't. I just kept replaying Wyn smashing into the cabinet over and over again. The shocked look on her face that shifted rapidly to pain . . .

I know it was the intruder who did this to her, but I couldn't help but feel like it was my fault. Wyn will probably shove that off my plate immediately when she listens to this, but.

She could have been really badly hurt. Wyn and even Max . . . they didn't do things like this before I came to Hollow Falls. I crash-landed in their lives and increased the amount of danger they were in by tenfold, like it didn't even matter.

People getting hurt because of my actions was bad enough, but to have it be Wyn? She's so important to me, I can't even find the words to describe it sometimes. There's this feeling in my chest, like a squeeze around my ribs when I think about her. And when I saw her hanging out with Ella this week—even though I know they've known each other forever—I feel weirdly . . . jealous?

I know I have no room to talk, what with the

whole Oly situation, but would it be too selfish if I said I wanted Wyn's attention? Like, all the time?

Ugh, this is probably way too personal for a true-crime podcast. And my feelings are hardly the highest priority right now. More important were the actual repercussions of what happened at Mr. Wyatt's house. Max had to go home feeling like he failed to protect his friends, and Wyn had a back full of glass. We also invaded a crime scene and got our fingerprints all over everything and broke a large cabinet that was definitely not broken the last time the police were in the building.

Even worse, the intruder managed to get away and we had no real clues as to his identity. And it was clear he was searching for the spyglass Mr. Wyatt had given me. If I hadn't known that the item had value before, I definitely did now. It wasn't unreasonable to think that Mr. Wyatt was killed for refusing to hand it over. He had barely managed to keep it from whoever killed him by passing it on to me, literally minutes before.

Before tonight, I had hidden the hollowed-out book in plain sight on the shelf in my room. But now I'd make sure that spyglass never left my side. This whole situation with The Hunt and the riddles was clearly related in some way to the spyglass, but I just can't figure out how. I need more information about how this all went down fifty years ago. I need to talk to my abuela.

I know they supposedly purged the library of everything related to the founder's treasure, but there has to be something . . . some small piece that was left behind that we can use to get the answers we need.

I won't stop looking until we find it.

Chapter 10

It had been less than twenty-four hours since the break-in. I could see anxious anger running through Max like I never had before. He jiggled his leg and clenched his jaw as he read, flipping the pages of the library book impatiently. We'd been in the library for about a half hour, but with Max acting like this, we really weren't getting much work done.

"It's not your fault, Max," Wyn whispered. She was sitting backward on her chair, leaning against the table to avoid putting pressure on her still-raw back. An unescapable reminder of what had happened.

He didn't look up from the table. "Maybe if he hadn't missed his punch at me, he wouldn't have swung at you, too."

"Maybe he shouldn't have broken into Mr. Wyatt's office, either," I shot back. "Wyn's going to be fine. Her back looked worse with her shirt on than it did with her shirt off. It was just a couple of scrapes. She was lucky the glass was as thick as it was, though. If it had *really* shattered, it could have been . . . worse."

Max sighed long and low, all the fight draining out of him like sand through a sieve. "It's more than that. You guys are my best friends, and I couldn't even protect you from one lousy cat burglar."

I thought about what Wyn had said yesterday. "Maybe not, but we're going to solve this mystery, find the founder's treasure, and figure out who we ran into at the house last night—and then you can go wild on them. I'll help."

"Me too," Wyn said with a grin.

Max raised an eyebrow. "You'll help?" he asked.

"I'll bring a bat and everything," she promised. "Scout's honor."

Max smirked and shook his head. "Okay. Well. Research is going pretty bad on my end. How about you guys?"

I looked around the library, but it was unsurprisingly pretty dead, considering it was a sunny Sunday morning. Still, I was cautious of how many people were supposedly out there looking for the exact same thing we were, and I lowered my voice all the same. I pushed my phone and the book I had open closer to Max, and Wyn scooted closer on my side.

"I'm going to record; I want to make sure we remember everything," I said, putting my recorder on the table and turning the volume way up to catch our whispering voices.

"As we figured out yesterday, the riddles are mostly literary. I think by figuring out how the founder made the answers correspond with places around town, it might be easier to understand the pattern. And maybe that will help us put all the pieces together," I said softly.

I pulled Wyn's map out from under an open book on the table and spread it out so we could see the writing.

Daniel is yet the father of this babe. Heaven. The Scarlet Letter.

What makes a monster and what makes a man? Hell. Frankenstein.

Treason and patriotism; wait and hope; time and silence. Hell. The Count of Monte Cristo.

The three solved riddles, in my abuela's spindly handwriting, were next to the church, the cemetery, and the jail, respectively.

"It looks like my abuela still had three riddles left to figure out. But there must be something else we're missing. The treasure probably isn't split up into six different locations. So how do all these places tie together?"

"Do you think the heaven/earth/hell thing has something

to do with it? Maybe it's all a misdirect and the treasure is just, like, at the church or something," Max suggested.

"I've been thinking about it, and my guess is that it's directional—telling you whether the clue is located up high, in the building's main area, or buried," I surmised. "And this town was founded in, like, 1850, so probably around when the riddles were written, it was a lot easier to figure out where something was hidden in a familiar building. Even if the clues are only up, middle, and down."

"Makes sense." Wyn shrugged and then flinched. The movement must have pulled the cuts on her back.

Max shot her a look of sympathy before looking back at the book in front of him. He scanned the open page again quickly and then pushed it closer to us, tapping at a paragraph with his finger.

"So, the only thing I've found that seems like it could be relevant is that by the 1930s, a lot of the town had been reconstructed and the older buildings demoed and rebuilt. Only four original buildings remained after 1960: the mayor's office, the bank, the post office, and the courthouse," he said. "But in the '80s, the mayor's office was rebuilt and the bank was majorly refurbished. And then last year, the post office burned down and had to be completely rebuilt as well. Which means the only building left from the town's creation is the courthouse."

"And I bet at least a few of those buildings changed physical locations between the original construction and the current one," Wyn added.

"I think I'm starting to understand how valuable an older map would be," I said, scanning the pages of Max's book. "You can hardly find the treasure if you're going to a courthouse that used to be a tannery or whatever."

"I mean, yeah. Most people aren't going to have a map this old lying around," Wyn said, tugging on the corner of Mr. Wyatt's map.

"That also makes sense why The Hunt was slightly more chill in the early 1900s," I said, thinking out loud. "The riddles are supposed to lead you to different locations. And at that time, some of those locations hadn't changed since the town was founded. It was only once things started being rebuilt that The Hunt became more difficult and more dangerous."

As I explained, Max's eyebrows got higher and higher.

"But there's still *something* we haven't figured out. Otherwise, someone in the last hundred and seventy years would have solved these riddles and claimed the treasure."

"They're all books, right?" Wyn pointed out. "*The Scarlet Letter*, *Frankenstein*, and *The Count of Monte Cristo*. If there's anything we know best, it's books. And we have the internet now, which is going to make this all a lot easier—shout-out to technology. Once we have that piece figured out, we can focus on the rest."

I nodded and pulled up the full list of riddles on my phone. I read out loud.

"'A dark night with bright stars.'"

Wyn typed into her phone. "Ooh, that one's almost a direct quote: *Crime and Punishment*," she said. "Next?"

"*Crime and Punishment* has got to be the police department, right?" Max interjected. "Or *maybe* the mayor's office, but I feel like these riddles are pretty heavy-handed so far."

"Like eight people in town probably had more than a high school education back then. Cut them some slack," Wyn joked.

A smile cracked Max's stony face at Wyn being well enough to try to make him laugh.

"'A great and terrible adventure of tradition and absurdity,'" I continued from the list.

"That one has to be—*Gulliver's Travels*. I freakin' hate that book by the way," Wyn said, looking down at her phone.

But when we tried the last one, we came up with nothing.

"'The eternal probable improbability, both divine and worldly, blood and bone over soil,'" I repeated the last riddle.

"The graveyard?" Wyn tried.

Max shook his head. "That's already the place for *Frankenstein.* We have to get the book first, and the rest of it will come easier."

"It's an old book, too," I reminded them. "So think of stuff that's old and famous and probably on every high school reading list."

"Why famous?" Max asked. "It could be any of a hundred thousand books."

"Books were extremely expensive and very few got truly well known in the way we think of them today. The founder was writing this for people in the future, which means that they were written with the understanding that the books they chose would still be relevant and stand the test of time. The other books were *The Scarlet Letter, Frankenstein, The Count of Monte Cristo.* Absolute giants of their time," I explained.

Max had his phone out and was tapping away wildly. "Here!" he said primly, handing it to me. "A giant list of books from 1600 to 1900."

I grimaced scrolling through the options.

"It could be religious, since it mentions divinity," Max suggested.

"Maybe, but it also says 'worldly,' so we're probably looking for something that mixes the two concepts into one. At the time I believe people felt that way about law, and medicine," I said.

"It mentions blood and bones, so maybe it's medical?" Wyn suggested.

"A 'probable improbability' could refer to the likelihood of dying or not," I said. "Maybe the hospital?"

Wyn sighed theatrically. "The only time I've heard about bone and soil is when my parents force me to go to church," she said. "Though that's probably not bookish enough of an answer."

I stopped scrolling and thought harder. "Man was made from dirt and woman . . . from a rib. 'Blood and bone over soil.' The book is about women. Women's 'probable improbability' . . . something women can do, but it's unlikely for them to be able to do . . ."

"Uh . . . back then? Basically everything," Wyn chipped in with a snort. "Being a woman before, like, 1970 was probably terrible. They had no rights at all."

I word searched the term "women," then "girls," then "woman." Nothing seemed right. Until . . .

"I . . . I think I found it," I said, zooming in on the screen. Wyn and Max leaned in close to read it.

"*A Vindication of the Rights of Women*, by Mary Wollstonecraft," Wyn breathed.

"The Goth Mother herself." I nodded. "Mary Shelley's mom."

Max shrugged. "Eh, the rest of the riddle is easy now. It's either the courthouse or the church. On the upper level somewhere since it said 'heaven.'"

"It's the courthouse," I said.

Wyn looked puzzled.

"The church was an answer to a previous riddle, and nothing else was used twice. Also, the courthouse is pretty much the only building in town that's still standing in its original location, mostly untouched," I explained.

"Yeah . . . Yeah, wow. We . . . Well. We did it," Wyn said, stunned. "Almost two hundred years of chaos, and we just . . . looked up the answers."

"Let's give ourselves a little more credit," Max said, tilting his head to the side. "That last one was a team effort."

I stood up and started packing up our stuff. "Back then, you probably had to have practically memorized all those books to recognize references like that when you saw them. That combined with the fact that most people probably couldn't even *afford* books, the people who created these riddles probably had an idea in mind of the kind of person who would be able to solve them.

"What we need to figure out now is more complicated

than that. We have Mr. Wyatt's old map, but we don't know how the spyglass comes into play here. And which of these locations we need to start with. But most importantly, we need to find out who killed Mr. Wyatt, and whether they did it to *find* the treasure or"—I paused for effect—"to keep people like us from finding it first."

Chapter 11

Wyn, Max, and I spent the rest of the weekend researching the town's founding and old spyglasses and anything we thought might lead us to Mr. Wyatt's killer. The one lead that would have really helped was talking to someone who knew him during The Hunt, but Abuela was still avoiding me.

Whenever I passed Abuela in the hallway or tried to start up a conversation during mealtime, she was blank. There hadn't been music playing when Abuela cooked or cleaned, and she began spending most of her free time alone in her room. The silence between us was a mutual thing, not the tenseness of when she was angry with me or I pushed her boundaries. But it was very clear that her grief came in the form of carefully withheld rage, not anguish or tears.

That's why I was so surprised to find Abuela waiting for me the next morning, dressed and ready for Mr. Wyatt's funeral.

But while she was no longer pretending she wasn't involved in what was going on, the ride to the church was still as silent as the last few days had been.

We didn't really go to church regularly, so it already felt weird being there for the funeral—cause of death notwithstanding. When we pulled up outside, it looked like the whole town had decided to show up. Cars of people attending the funeral were lined around the block. I had almost forgotten the street could look like that. It was rare that there was anyone parked on the street in Hollow Falls. There simply weren't enough residents.

I breathed in the scent of Abuela's perfume and sighed. She sat stiffly next to me, expressionless and cold, as she looked for parking. For the funeral, Abuela had dressed in gray, not black. It was strange to see the color on her. It might have been the only gray dress she had. She had also combed her curly hair into a severe bun on the top of her head, leaving a few tendrils down around her face. It made her look like a younger version of herself. I thought about saying so, but every time I gathered the courage to start a conversation, the look on her face always made me reconsider.

We finally found a place to park and made our way up the block to the church.

"Are you all right?" I asked Abuela gently as we got close enough to be among other people heading inside.

She shook her head. "No. I will be soon, though."

Abuela climbed the front stairs and strode confidently into the church. I followed her inside, peering around on my tiptoes to see if I could find Max and Wyn. I pulled out my phone and sent a quick text in the group chat.

Tig:

Where are you?

Max:

At the back in the corner.

Wyn:

Don't even bother looking for a pew. They're all filled up. There are some assigned seats near the front, but my family is in the back by the doorway.

I put my arm out to guide Abuela forward, and we stepped into the main space of the church. Wyn had been right: it was packed. As we headed down the aisle, I noticed that we were getting some looks. Most people who were here for Mr. Wyatt's funeral were minding their business, but every so often, an older person would spot Abuela and either raise their eyebrows in shock or a sneer. Abuela kept her eyes forward and didn't acknowledge any of these glances.

There were chairs in front of the closest pews to the casket, arranged in tight rows to fit more people, and just as Wyn had said, there were names on a few of them. I spotted Wyn and her parents in the corner, clearly not included in the select honored guests who'd received a seat up front.

Max was in line to see the casket. He'd never gotten to meet Mr. Wyatt when he was alive.

As we made our way past the aisle leading up to the line, a tall man nearly as old as Mr. Wyatt looked down at Abuela furiously.

"What are you doing here?" he spat, his eyes narrowing in distaste. "It's a bit late for recompensation."

"Mind your business," Abuela replied sternly.

Then, after a second of contemplation, she tugged her arm out of mine.

"I'm sorry, mija, but I have something I must do," she said before striding off, purposefully. I watched her head toward the casket, weaving her way through the crowd.

"Tig!" Wyn called, waving me over. Max got out of line to come join us, and he was also almost back to Wyn's side.

"How are things at home?" Wyn asked after pulling me into a quick hug.

"Hard to tell," I said, glancing over my shoulder at Abuela still pushing her way to the front of the space. "Abuela is acting really out of character. Today is the first she's acknowledged what happened on Friday. But she still won't let me ask her about any of it."

"Her hair looks really good, though!" Max said quietly. "I know this is supposed to be a sad event, but that bun slaps."

"Yeah," I said dubiously, "the bun seems more like a symptom of being reminded of her past or something rather than a bold new fashion choice."

Wyn's mom, standing behind her, beautiful and tall, closed her eyes and shook her head. "Cut her some slack. Grief makes strangers of us all."

"Are you going to go look at the body?" Max asked me once Wyn's mom had looked away. "He looks really weird and bad. His skin is all . . ."

"All dead people look gross. And the poor guy fell out of a window," Wyn pointed out.

"No, I mean he looks . . . He's got a lot of makeup on, but it's kind of sliding off and underneath his skin is all bluish."

"Hmm," I said. "That doesn't really line up with death by fall, does it?" Could someone have killed Mr. Wyatt *before* throwing him to his death? "I'll definitely take a closer look later. It looks like the service is starting."

Mr. Green, who was at the front of the church, cleared his throat.

"Thank you all for joining us today. Before we begin, we would like to hear from a few people who knew Alan Wyatt," he said, his voice wavering. "Please form a line to the right of the first pew." He then reached down to help the first speaker step up to the riser—Abuela.

Wyn, Max, and I exchanged looks. Maybe this funeral would be more informative than expected.

"Good afternoon, all," Abuela's voice rang out crisp and strong.

"How dare you come here!" someone in the congregation hissed.

With an authoritative scowl, Mr. Green crossed his arms, clearly championing her presence. But the heckler in the audience was far from the only one unsupportive of Abuela being allowed to speak. The man who had burst into Mr. Wyatt's office, Franklin Baker, was also at the front of the room. He seemed nearly apoplectic that Abuela was here, his face red with anger. Some of the members that I remembered sneering at us in the foyer were beginning to speak in angry, hushed tones among themselves.

"Good afternoon," Abuela repeated. "I know many of you are surprised that I am here." She paused as if waiting for more interruptions. "But you shouldn't be surprised. I walked beside Alan Wyatt long before many of you were even born. We battled together and laughed together. He was there for me in some of the darkest moments of my life."

Abuela's eyes flicked to find Noel, perched on the edge of her seat, about halfway back in the church. But before I could point it out to Max and Wyn, Abuela was facing the crowd again.

"Alan was a giant among men," Abuela continued. "He was fierce, cunning, relentless, and kind. His impact in this community will echo beyond the indignity of his death."

Abuela stopped and looked out at the crowd.

"Some of you are here to pay respects to a great man. Maybe you knew him, maybe you only knew of him. Regardless, I am glad that you are here. He deserved many faces to see him to his rest.

"Some of you, on the other hand, have been jackals in his midst, wolves in his woods, and have come to gloat at the feast of his bones. You, who cast eyes at me for my silence and distance, while the sin of greed tears your own souls to shreds.

"No matter what you've heard to the contrary, this was an unnatural death. And as much as it pains to discuss the violence of his passing, denying it spits in the face of justice. Alan deserved more."

She paused again, then said very slowly and clearly, "And lastly, to his killer—because there is no doubt in my heart that they are among us—I know what you are looking for. What you took Alan from this world to get. And I will make sure you never, ever find it."

At the mention of a killer in the room, the mourners all began looking around fearfully and murmuring among themselves.

"Thank you for your time, and my sincerest condolences," Abuela finished.

Mr. Green helped her down from the riser, his hand gentle and familiar on her arm. He walked with her through the crowd, sharply eyeing anyone who tried to approach her so that Abuela could move freely.

"Holy shit," I said, looking back at Wyn and Max. "What the hell was that?"

"I don't know, but she's coming this way," Max said anxiously.

Abuela was indeed making her way toward us, Mr. Green still in tow.

"It's nice to see you, Mr. and Mrs. Abbott," she said to Wyn's parents, then turned to me. "I'm going to go sit in the pews on the second floor, as it's clear that I'm unwelcome down here and I do not want to interrupt the others from their mourning. When you are ready to leave, come upstairs and find me."

Then she turned on her heel and walked briskly toward the staircase. Mr. Green nodded at us kindly, then went off back toward the front of the room.

"You're right. She is . . . acting different," Wyn said, grimacing.

"When your grandmother passed, I watched *It's a Wonderful Life* on repeat for three full days," Wyn's father, a stout and gentle-faced man, said. "Give her some time, and it will get better."

He squeezed my shoulder reassuringly, and all of a sudden, I had an uncharacteristic pang of longing for my own dad. He probably wouldn't have said or done anything like Wyn's father but . . . it suddenly hit me how hard it was to be alone with someone else's grief.

"I'm going to go to the bathroom," I said, needing a moment to decompress. "Then do you want to go to the reception area? People are still kind of staring in our direction."

"Oh!" Wyn brightened. "Yeah, we went there for a second

earlier. They have brownies!" she said with entirely too much enthusiasm for a funeral.

"There's a bathroom on this floor on the other side of the church kitchen," Wyn's father said.

"Thanks," I replied, darting away.

While the church auditorium was full, no one was near the hallway leading to the restrooms, which was definitely a relief. I decided to cut through the kitchen, and as I opened the door, I could smell the lingering scent of appetizers that had been heated up in here.

To my surprise, I wasn't alone.

Judah was rummaging rather aggressively through the drawers, clearly looking for something.

"Hey," I said.

He whirled around in surprise, but when he saw it was me, he visibly relaxed. "Hey, Tig. Nice to see you. Are you enjoying . . . ? Well, 'enjoying' might not be the right word. Are you having an okay time?"

"At a funeral?" I said, not giving him the break he so clearly needed. Then I gasped. "What the hell happened to your face?"

Judah had a large bruise on the side of his cheek that he'd covered only semi-successfully with makeup. At my mention of it, his hand flew up to the bruise in a panic, but he caught himself and laughed sheepishly. He closed the drawer he'd been ransacking and leaned back against the counter.

"I'm not as graceful as I would like to be. Right after I dropped you guys off at the library, I tripped in the dark and fell down a couple stairs. I was checking out the damage in the bathroom when Mr. Wyatt . . . you know. So I missed all the chaos," he said, shrugging. "I'm just glad my cheekbone didn't get broken." He touched his face again. "I'm not that great at makeup, but it seemed rude to show up to a funeral and make it all about my busted mug."

"You've got that right. Anyway, what were you looking for?" I asked. "Maybe I could help?"

Judah laughed and rolled his eyes, holding up a frayed sleeve of his ill-fitting suit. "Ugh, scissors. I didn't want to bother the church staff; they seem busy enough. Don't we all keep our scissors in a kitchen drawer these days? I would use a knife, but I always feel super weird savagely hacking away at stuff instead of just cutting it. That kind of violence is not my style."

A frisson of alarm sparked in my chest.

"What kind of violence *is* your style?" I asked archly.

He leaned forward with a smirk and cupped his hand around his mouth as if he was telling a secret. "Violence of the pen. Books are the closest humanity has gotten to immortality,

Tig. You slander someone good enough on paper, you slander them forever."

"Ha ha," I said dryly. "You know what I meant."

Judah winked and turned back around to resume his search. In spite of myself, I felt my cheeks heating up. Now I could understand why Wyn had felt the way she did about him. He was charming and clever. Judah crouched down and started opening up the larger cabinets.

"I know you didn't come all this way to talk to me. Even though chatting with you is a delight," he said cheekily, his head deep inside the cabinetry. "Where were you headed?"

"Oh," I said, disarmed. "Things were getting a bit hectic out there, and I just needed somewhere to clear my head. I was looking for the bathroom."

"Well." He sat back on his heels and looked up at me. "You're almost there actually. It's down the hall and to the right. Before you go, though . . . when are you available to hang out? I'd still love to pick your brain."

The way he said it . . . Was he asking me out? I couldn't really tell with him. He seemed to have flirtiness as his default personality. But it was incredibly weird to hit on someone at a funeral . . .

Judah tossed his hair out of his eyes, waiting patiently for my answer. Even though he looked nothing like him, the gesture reminded me a bit of Oly. It wasn't often that guys looked at me with so much interest, so I couldn't help but think about the last one who did. Instantly I felt a bit queasy and a little guilty.

"Actually, I was supposed to hook back up with Wyn and Max. I wasted my bathroom run time in here. I'm sure they're waiting for me."

Judah shrugged. "No problem. Just . . . text me if you want. I'm not going to be in town for long, though, I don't think. If everything works out, I'll be headed to Stanford in a couple weeks."

"Oh man, congratulations!" I said genuinely, beginning to back out of the room. "I'll see you later, Judah. I won't forget to text."

"You better not!" he called out right before the door to the kitchen closed.

I rubbed my cheeks and took a deep breath. There was just too much going on right now for me to belatedly process my emotions about the whole Oly situation with some random new guy.

I strode back across the foyer to Max and Wyn, who were sitting at the foot of the stairs.

"Are you okay?" Max asked. "Your face is all red and splotchy."

"To be honest, no, I'm not," I admitted, silently hoping that Judah hadn't been seeing whatever version of my face Max was currently staring at. "But we should head upstairs and grab Abuela before going to the cemetery. I'm sure she'll be glad to have something to eat, too. Then we can all get out of here as soon as possible. I feel like Abuela might be a little more responsive to my questions after all this."

Max looked doubtful, but he didn't press me to talk about it anymore while the three of us climbed the stairs. The hallways were bright and musty—the light from the stained-glass windows tinting everything in oranges and greens.

We emerged onto the second floor, high up above the pews, almost level with the giant chandelier. There was a chest-high wall that wrapped around the open space. You could see over it, but it was definitely hard to imagine falling down; you'd have to hoist yourself up on purpose. I wasn't a fan of heights, especially after the events last year, so I was glad for it. The pews around us were empty except for Abuela. She was staring out a stained-glass window, angry and resolute.

"Abuela?" I called. She looked up but didn't rise to leave. Max and Wyn, understanding that perhaps this was a private moment, gave me a relieved glance, and both descended the stairs together. I made my way over to Abuela alone.

"How are you doing?" I asked gently.

"I'm . . ." Abuela sighed. "I could be better."

I peered over the edge of the balcony and looked down at Mr. Wyatt lying in his casket. From this view, I could see the full length of him. Max was right—his face did look strangely blue. I remembered the way he fell, his entire body rigid before collapsing to a heap. I'd been pretty certain Mr. Wyatt didn't just *happen* to fall from a window after giving me a secret spyglass connected to some generations-long treasure hunt, but this cemented my theory.

"Abuela," I said slowly. "I think Mr. Wyatt was poisoned. I think someone snuck into the library after Wyn and I left, poisoned him, and then hurled his body through the window so they could escape in the pandemonium after he hit the ground."

Abuela covered her eyes. "I don't need this right now, Tig."

"Aren't you listening?" I said urgently. "I know someone killed Mr. Wyatt—and I think I know why—but I don't have any leads. The last conversation he had was one where he was trying to tell me and Wyn how to find the founder's treasure—to end The Hunt once and for all.

"Clearly you knew this man and knew him well. Is there anyone down there that you think could have done this?"

"I'm warning you, Tig, I don't want to talk about this," Abuela said forcefully.

"But what if he's not the first?" I exclaimed. "What if it's Levinson all over again and more people are going to die? If you help me catch the killer *now* instead of just sitting here, full of secrets, then maybe we'll have less to cry about later."

"MARGARET TORRES!" Abuela shouted, louder than I'd ever heard her before. I stopped talking immediately and stared back at her with shock. Her face was dark with fury, and her hands were clenched into fists. The noise downstairs quieted for a moment as her voice echoed through the church. Abuela closed her eyes and took a deep breath.

"I asked you nicely, but now I'm demanding. If you press me about this again, I cannot be held responsible for what I will say," she said, much quieter. "And if you care about me at all, you will leave this church and find your own way home."

"I'm sorry," I murmured, devastated. Abuela had never spoken to me this way.

"I know," Abuela said. "But I need a moment to grieve. Alan . . . he was like my Max. Noel was my Wyn. Think about how . . . about how you would *feel* if . . . Just *think* about it, Tig, and give me a break."

Her voice was thick, the words coming out in fits and starts, and I immediately felt ashamed.

"I'll see you at home," I replied. "I'm sorry."

I trudged down the stairs, dreading facing the rest of the

congregation, which had heard me get reprimanded. To my surprise, Noel was leaning against the wall next to the stairs.

She looked up as I made my way all the way down.

"There's a side exit to your right if you go down that hall," she said gently. An olive branch if I ever saw one.

"Thanks," I said, and roughly wiped my eyes before any tears managed to find their way out.

Noel cleared her throat. "I heard . . . that you have some questions. I would like to give you the time and space to ask them. If you're not busy later today, feel free to swing by," she said. "Bring your friends; they're both welcome."

It was unexpected, this kindness from Noel. Her eyes darted up the stairwell, and I realized that she was waiting for me to go so she could join her friend.

"Oh . . . uh. Thanks. I think we will," I said.

Noel smiled gently, and it transformed her face. For a moment, I could see how she must have looked when she was the most important person in Abuela's life.

Chapter 12

After the funeral, I dragged Max and Wyn with me to the Star Diner. I wasn't ready to face home—not after my fight with Abuela—and we needed to kill time until Noel was ready to answer our questions.

When I told Max and Wyn what Abuela said upstairs at the church and then what Noel said afterward, both of them immediately agreed to come along. They seemed as upset as I was about how Abuela was dealing with this. And we all wanted to get to the bottom of whatever was going on before anyone else got hurt. (Wyn thought we didn't notice her wincing every time she turned too fast or raised her arms too high. We noticed.)

Finally, after a few hours of moping around the diner and more cups of coffee than we could count,

I checked my watch. "Let's go," I said flatly.

We trudged to the bus stop together. Max and Wyn bickered softly, but let me sit in silence. Their banter relaxed me a little. It felt so normal and trivial that I could almost forget that my abuela couldn't stand the sight of me right now and that someone had nearly killed my friend two days ago.

"So, do we trust Noel?" Wyn asked tentatively as we got off the bus at our stop. "She's obviously wrapped up in all this, but what if she's playing us? What if she had something to do with Mr. Wyatt's death?"

I sighed. "Honestly, I don't know. But at least she's finally giving us something to go on."

"Oh!" Max said suddenly. "I think that might be her house all the way down at the end of the block."

The neighborhood had whittled down from houses right off the sidewalk, to houses with a short walk-up garden path like Mr. Wyatt's, and finally, at the very edge of the residential area, houses built for privacy. From the sidewalk, you could only see wrought-iron fences and lush greenery, the homes far back from the property line, at the end of winding driveways.

"I think I've only been in this neighborhood once before," Wyn said, ogling the sculptural hedges through the fences. "Back when I was delivering pizzas. They wouldn't even let me go inside the fence; they sent some butler guy to get the pizza."

"That's pretty typical of rich people." I shrugged. "There doesn't seem to be a ton of them in Hollow Falls, but every town has them. In New York, the richest ones don't even let regular people get this close to their homes. They all live in high-rises in the clouds above everyone else."

When we finally arrived at the address listed on Noel's card, I noticed her spiked fence seemed simpler than those of her neighbors. But on closer inspection, the points at the top of each spire weren't pyramids at all; they were tiny crows. Max snapped a quick picture on his phone. I approached the gate, which had a security keypad next to it. There was a place to enter in a code, but there hadn't been anything else written on the card. Instead, I rang the bell.

The keypad gave off a soft hum in G. Then, to all of our surprise, a bell near the gate rang in the same tone. Farther down the path, we could hear another bell ring, then another, until the noise faded off into the distance. After thirty seconds of silence, I reached out to ring the bell again, but before my fingers touched the keypad, the speaker crackled to life.

"Hello?" Noel's voice sounded a bit harried—like we had caught her at a bad time, even though *she* was the one who had invited *us*.

"It's Tig Torres," I said loudly.

There was some kind of racket before she answered. "I'm glad you made it. I'll be right down."

The speaker went dead, and the gate unlocked with a loud clunking sound. Max, Wyn, and I pushed into the garden and closed the gate firmly behind us.

"Wow," Wyn said. "She must really like birds."

That was an understatement.

The gardens beyond the gate had been tastefully obscured by tall hedges, so we were unable to see until we were fully inside. Noel's front walkway was a veritable maze of local plant life, tall grass rolling wildly, kept in check by a tangle of brambly bushes that left the stone pathway clear. The trees on the property were dense and low to the ground, thickly hung with birdhouses of all shapes and sizes painted a tasteful black lacquer.

All of which would be completely fine—normal even—if not for the hundreds of crows sitting in the trees and walking on the ground.

"Are those mirrors?" Max screeched. He jerked back from a bird that had come to pick at his shoelace. It squawked angrily and took flight away from him. "What is it with this stupid town and mirrors?!" he shouted.

"Well. Corvids like shiny things," I said, curiously watching it as it joined the rest of the birds in the trees. "Someone who appreciates corvids would know that. Your horrendous mirror experience aside, I think it's cool."

"I like it. It's kind of Goth," Wyn remarked. "And not in the whole death-metal, platform-boot way. In the Mary Shelley, Sisters of Mercy way."

"Well, I think it's creepy. It smells like birdseed and hamsters out here," Max grouched, hopping out of the way of another bird that seemed interested in the piece of fabric hanging at the bottom of his jeans.

"Corvids are really smart. Be nice to them and they'll remember you forever," I replied. "I've also read that if you're mean to them, they never forget."

"That's not less creepy; that just made them creepier," Max whined. "Can we just go inside as quickly as possible?"

Wyn slung an arm over his shoulder. "Don't worry, I'll protect you."

As we got closer to the house, I noticed the bells lining the walkway that had passed on the doorbell chime. They were brass and enclosed in a small cage with a little hammer to strike them. They were on the same pike as the walkway lights, which were artfully designed to look like old-fashioned candle lamps.

After a few minutes of walking through twists and turns

on the path that completely obscured the structure from street view, we finally saw Noel's house.

"Oh my god," Max said. "What does she do for a living? Being a true-crime enthusiast *cannot* be this lucrative."

It wasn't much bigger than Mr. Wyatt's, but it was an entirely unique style. While Mr. Wyatt's house had been a colonial mansion, Noel's house was a painted lady: a Victorian style known for elaborate bright paint. It had probably been built around the time of the town's conception. I'd seen a few when I'd gone on vacation in San Francisco a few summers back, but Noel's blew them out of the water.

Unlike most Victorian painted ladies, which were colorful, Noel's home was gray from the top to the bottom, just like she was gray. It had been painted dark gray near the roof, transitioning to a gray so light it was close to white at the base. There was no distinction for windows or lintels, stonework, or decoration; it was just steady color gradient all the way down. The shutters were either painted wood, matching the exterior, or they were similarly painted pull-down shades. The entire house gave one the impression of standing at the edge of a cliff overlooking the ocean on a foggy day. The only thing on the entire house that wasn't gray was the door.

It was a velvety, light-sucking pitch black.

"She kind of looks like her own house," I commented. "But I

wouldn't mention that to her. Who knows how she'll take it."

"I can't wait to get inside," Wyn said, practically skipping up the path. "I bet her interior design is just as incredible."

"I bet she has the kind of couches that make you anxious to spill things on them." I smirked.

"I just hope there aren't any birds inside, too," Max said anxiously.

There wasn't a knocker, so I raised my hand to rap on the black wood, but before my knuckles could hit the door, it was tugged open.

"Thank you for coming." Noel was wearing a dark gray sweater and light gray slacks. Like she had during the funeral and the Murder of Crows meeting, she wore high spiked stiletto heels, even though she was in her own house. She stepped to the side and held the door open as we filed inside.

Just like the outside, the inside was decorated in shades of gray. The decor was plush and feminine. The carpet was so lush my shoes sunk in with every step. Noel guided us to the living room, where she had set out a tea set with four places.

"Earl Grey." She nodded. "I hope that's acceptable."

"Thank you," we chorused in unison, awkwardly.

"I'm certain you're eager for answers," Noel said. "Especially considering Sofia's outburst at the funeral this morning."

"She won't tell me anything," I said in a rush. "Obviously

you guys were friends when you were younger, and she was clearly involved in The—" I paused, not wanting to give away our hand. Wyn was right. We *didn't* know what Noel's angle was. "In the Murder of Crows," I finished.

If Noel noticed my hesitation, she didn't comment on it.

"Sofia and I were . . . close when we were younger. There was a time that I would have followed her anywhere. She was headstrong and brave, and I just liked being in the warmth of her shadow. We were . . . companions."

I could feel Wyn shift, and suddenly her shoe was pinching against the side of mine hard. I nudged her back to let her know I definitely understood. I had been getting some weird vibes ever since Abuela rejected Noel's offer to meet. Then there had been the way Abuela looked at her during the funeral. But there was so much else going on that I hadn't really had time to think about what it all meant.

But now that Noel had put words to it, it was hard to miss. It also made a lot of other things slot into place. The poetry, the anger. Abuela and Noel weren't acting like best friends who had a falling-out. They were acting like exes who had a bad breakup.

What a chaotic realization. Max coughed dryly and quickly took a gulp of his steaming tea. I glanced over at him briefly, and he looked like he was using all the restraint in his body not to smirk.

"I was so angry with Sofia for some of the decisions she made," Noel continued obliviously. "But the heart just . . . can't take being pulled in two directions. As much as I cared for her, I was always going to be tempted by something else—somewhere she wouldn't follow me.

"When we realized our . . . friendship was at an impasse, we agreed not to see each other again. We knew it would just dredge up old pain and remind us of how much we had lost. And I kept my word. I haven't spoken to your grandmother in fifty years—until today."

Noel blinked repeatedly, as if to clear the emotion from her eyes. Then she suddenly let out a wet chuckle. "The time we've wasted spent on opposite sides of this place."

"The town or ideologically speaking?" I couldn't help but ask.

Noel let out another peal of laughter, but this one sounded a little more lighthearted. Like talking about this again after so long was healing to her. Like her offering to answer our questions wasn't just for our benefit.

"Both. With her it was always both. And when we met Alan and Charlie—Mr. Wyatt and Mr. Green—we all had such a golden summer together. Alan was so handsome and ruthless back then."

I remembered the photos we had seen of him in the *Talon*

yearbook. I could imagine he made quite the impression.

"We were all looking for something—competing to see which team would find it first," Noel continued. "We played a game of cat and mouse until we realized that we might be more successful if we worked together."

"The founder's treasure," Wyn chimed in.

Noel nodded slowly. "I wondered how much you knew."

"Mr. Wyatt told us," I admitted. "The night of the meeting, he asked for our help looking for it—so he could get rid of the temptation and end the violence."

A flicker of irritation crossed Noel's eyes, but it was gone as suddenly as it appeared.

"What can you tell us about the early days of The Hunt?"

Noel closed her eyes in memory. "People had been actively searching for the founder for a long time, but everything really began to come to a head in the late '60s and early '70s.

"Sofia and I met at the library while both independently doing research on the riddles, and we decided to team up. Alan and Charlie noticed that we were getting close, and they started trying to intimidate us into stopping—or to hand over the information we had. Apparently, we were the closest anyone had gotten since the 1930s. By then, the last person who knew the actual location of the founder's treasure had died, and unfortunately, they had taken that information with them. So it was truly anyone's game."

Noel paused to think for a bit before continuing. "We were all so . . . young back then. It was easy for me, Sofia, Charlie, and Alan to go from mortal enemies to grudging rivals to shaky friends, and finally become true companions. By the time we started working together, we had independently solved nearly all the riddles, but we knew there was another piece we needed to find to lead us to the actual treasure. An artifact that no one else had discovered before."

"The spyglass!" I said, leaning forward.

But before Noel could respond, a telephone pealed from deep within the house. "I must get that," Noel said, standing up quickly. "I'll be right back."

I gazed after her to make sure she was gone.

"Tig!" Wyn said, but I hushed her quickly. "She could still hear us." I pulled out my phone. Immediately Wyn and Max took theirs out, too, and started typing furiously.

Wyn:

WLW Abuela?!?!?!?!?

Tig:

I KNOW, I'M SCREAMING INTERNALLY.

Max:

Did you know about this? Does your dad? What about your grandpa??

Tig:

She's literally never mentioned it, so probably not? But like, WTF.

Wyn:

I am LOSING my MIND.

Tig:

How do you think I feel!!!

Max:

IT'S VERY CUTE.

Tig:

I feel like Abuela would kill you if she heard you say that.

Wyn:

DO YOU THINK THEY'VE KISSED?

Tig:

Wyn, please.

Max:

lolololol

Tig:

We can talk about this later, but right now we gotta focus.

We've got to get Noel to tell us how the spyglass works. But don't let her know we have it.

I don't like NOT trust her, but I also don't TRUST trust her. You know?

Wyn:

Fine. But we ARE coming back to this. AT LENGTH.

Max:

Oh, for sure.

Noel came striding back into the room right as we all tucked our phones back away. She looked a bit more like her normal, serious self. The softness she'd shown when talking about Abuela seemingly wiped away by whoever she'd spoken to on the phone.

"Sorry about that," she said, looking at us with a forced smile.

"You were telling us about an artifact?" I asked forcefully. "So even if one has, theoretically, solved all the riddles, you still couldn't find the treasure?"

"It's unlikely. The riddles all point to places in town—which I'm sure you've figured out already. But the location of the actual treasure can only be seen on a specific map, created by the ones who hid the founder's treasure in the first place," Noel said. "And that map, I have on good authority, is kept under lock and key by our own Mr. Green."

"Why him?" Wyn asked, putting her elbows on her knees and leaning forward.

Noel shrugged. "When we had our falling-out and Alan arranged to have The Hunt all but wiped from existence, he and Mr. Green worked together to keep the artifacts separate—so that no one would be able to find the treasure without their cooperation. Selfish old men," Noel spat, something ugly flashing across her face.

"So Charlie took the map and Alan took possession of the

spyglass. If there was another piece in Sofia's care, they didn't deign to tell me. But I do know you need all the pieces in order to solve it." She took a drink of her tea and sighed.

"That's quite a jump from working together to them locking you out of The Hunt," I said slowly, not wanting to push Noel too much. "What happened between you guys?"

"The whole search came to an end not long after a man named Jet Cassidy died. He was looking for one of the clues in the church, and he fell three stories to his death. Jet's death brought us together, but in a way it also tore us apart." She paused. "It is odd how many people fall in this town . . ."

"Yeah," I agreed, a tingle going up my spine. "I wonder if that string of coincidences is in Judah's book. He can add his own trip down the stairs," I said, trying to lighten the mood.

Noel made a strange expression. "What?"

"Judah busted up his face on Friday night. That's why he wasn't around when Mr. Wyatt fell. He was doing first aid in the bathroom."

Noel raised an eyebrow. "Judah was there when the police arrived to take out the body. He wasn't hurt at all. He must have fallen somewhere else."

A thrum of fear went up the back of my spine. I turned to Wyn. "Judah said he tripped after he dropped us off at the library. Did you run into him at all after that? When you were taking up the cake?"

Wyn nodded her head slowly. "I did see him on my way upstairs, but he was coming out of a hallway on the second floor, not from Mr. Wyatt's office. We both reached the landing around the same time, but he ran off in a different direction. He looked fine . . ." She trailed off.

Max stood up. "That rat bastard," he seethed.

Noel looked up at him, scandalized at his outburst. Max visibly remembered that there was no way in hell he could explain his reaction to Noel.

Because if Judah didn't hurt his face the way he said he did, he must have hurt it another time.

Like when Max pushed him against the cabinet in Mr. Wyatt's office when we all broke in on Saturday night.

When he was ransacking the dead man's library looking for the spyglass.

Chapter 13

I steered a seething Max toward the door of Noel's house as Wyn trailed behind me. "We just remembered we're late for another interview—*Talon* business," I called to our host over my shoulder. "Thanks for the tea."

As the door closed behind us, Max set off at a furious pace down Noel's long walkway.

"Judah works at the convenience store a half mile away," Max said with an intensity I had never heard from him before.

I jogged behind him. "Don't you think we should maybe make a plan?" I panted. Max's legs were much longer than they were last year, and I had never been more aware of it.

"I'm mostly planning to fight him until the cops pull me off him," Max said resolutely. "What's your plan?"

"Dude, slow down!" Wyn begged. He did not slow down,

and instead, he continued to stride purposefully, turning sharply left at the end of Noel's street.

"But Judah is obviously in on The Hunt. What if he has some information we can get from him?" I said.

"We can get the information after I get in one solid punch," Max said. He continued to walk in silence the rest of the way. Wyn and I kept exchanging nervous glances and did our best to keep up.

A few minutes later, Max yanked open the door of the convenience store where Judah worked.

The bells at the top jangled wildly behind Max as he approached the front counter. A woman who looked like she wished she could be anywhere else was sitting on a stool, chewing gum and looking bored. She perked up in alarm as we got closer.

"Welcome to Sparky-Mart, can I help you?" she squeaked.

"Where's Judah?" Max demanded.

"He's not working today. Maybe I can get him a message from you later?" the woman tried, but Max shook his head.

"Do you know where we can find him?" I asked gently, aware that Max was starting to freak this woman out. "We need to speak to him as soon as possible. Lives are at stake."

The cashier looked really conflicted.

"I . . . don't know his home address, but here's a white

pages book. You can look it up yourself. His mom's name is Gina."

Max snatched the book and flipped through it quickly. Wyn made awkward eye contact with the cashier, then put a candy bar on the counter.

"Thank you for this, and sorry," she said, pulling her wallet out of the back pocket of her jeans.

"Judah seems like a nice guy," the cashier said to me and Wyn, ringing up the purchase. "But most men do, I guess. I hope everything turns out okay."

Wyn dropped her change in the tip jar and grimaced.

"Yeah, me too."

"Got it." Max took a picture of the page with his phone and headed briskly toward the door.

"Have a good day!" the cashier called behind us.

Judah's house was small and a bit run-down. The lawn was filled with scraggly weeds and the paint was peeling off the siding. Max marched up to the door and knocked hard.

"Who is it?" I could hear a woman shout. Then I heard Judah answer her: "It's probably the mailman; I ordered something. One second!"

My heart began racing as the door unlocked and swung open. I didn't get more than a glimpse of Judah before it swung closed again, but it was enough for Wyn and Max to see Judah's bruised face—just like I had at the funeral that morning.

I was hit with a pang of guilt. I should have put the pieces together as soon as I saw him. Instead I let him smooth-talk me into thinking the injury was just a coincidence. But the bruise was glaring proof that we had indeed encountered him two nights ago, and from the panic in his eyes, he knew he'd been caught.

Before the door could shut all the way, Max shoved his foot into the house and slammed his palm against the jamb. I helped, pushing the door hard with my shoulder, and we tumbled into his house.

"I'm sorry!" he said at once, backing away into the hallway. "It's not my fault!"

"What do you mean, it's not your fault?!" I shouted, pushing him so hard that he banged against the wall.

Judah cringed back. "I mean, yeah, I admit it. It's my fault Wyn got hurt, but—"

"But what?!" Max roared. "She's smaller than you. You could have killed her!"

"I'm right here," Wyn said, rolling her eyes and closing the door softly behind us.

"I—I know. It's no excuse, but I'm being blackmailed. I didn't even want to be there!" Judah shouted back.

"You—what?" Max yelled, this time in confusion.

Judah shook his head; his face was starting to get red with panic.

"Judah? Are you okay?" a voice that had to belong to his mom called from upstairs. Judah put up his finger, gesturing for us to be quiet.

"Yeah, Mom, just some noise from outside," he yelled.

He turned back to us. "She's using a breathing machine. None of this is her fault, so please. Just . . . come to my room and you can do whatever you want there."

Max was angry, but he wasn't a bad person. I could see him warring internally with giving Judah his just deserts right in the hallway versus having to wait a few minutes.

"Fine," he said.

We followed Judah to his bedroom in the finished basement. He closed the door and made sure we could see that it wasn't locked before he began talking.

"I am so sorry I pushed you into that hutch, Wyn, but I'm in a really bad place, and I just got desperate."

Wyn crossed her arms over her chest and glared.

"Who is blackmailing you—and why?" I interrupted.

"I don't know," Judah admitted. "A year ago, around when

I was starting to apply to colleges, I got a notification that one of our overdue bills had been paid in full. Things haven't been the best since my dad died, and my mom has been ill as long as I can remember. At the time, I was just so grateful and relieved that I didn't question it. Then a few of our other debts were paid, and eventually all our bills were being handled. I asked my mom if she knew anyone who would do this for us, and she said she thought it could be a mistake or charity of some kind and that if I pressed the companies, they might get suspicious and reverse the charges, and then we'd be in more debt than ever."

Judah looked embarrassed to be admitting all this, but he was clearly too scared of Max's balled fists to stop talking.

"Then, one day, I got a letter asking me to do something. It wasn't signed, so I thought it was a prank and ignored it. Within a month our electricity bill hadn't been paid, and I quickly understood that this situation wasn't a 'gift'; it was transactional. I've been doing stuff for whoever it is ever since."

"Don't you have a job?" Max asked coldly.

"I also go to school full-time," Judah reminded him. "All my money goes to groceries and medication. This would have been the first year that I was able to get a full-time job instead."

"But you told me you were going to college soon . . ." I said dubiously.

"Yes. That's it exactly. I was told to find some spyglass in exchange for my blackmailer paying for college. A full ride," he said firmly. "I got into Stanford, Tig. No one in my entire family has ever gotten anything more than a high school education. Don't look down on me for this. Look around. What would you do?"

"But you didn't find it," I said, not looking away from his guilty, bruised face.

Judah sighed. "You know that I didn't."

"Do you know what it was even going to be used for?" I tried. "Why your blackmailer wanted it so badly?"

Judah shook his head. "Someone starts blackmailing you and you tend not to ask questions," he said, rubbing his fingers through his hair in distress.

I looked at Wyn and Max. Wyn raised her eyebrows, and Max—though still furious—shrugged one shoulder roughly. Judah definitely wasn't going on our Christmas card lists, but it seemed like we were all buying his story.

And if Judah didn't know about The Hunt or have anything to do with it, that meant we were back to square one. Again.

Max huffed in disgust and crossed his arms, but the wind had been let out of our sails. I finally stopped and took the time to look around. The wallpaper in the room was so old it was stained yellow. The corners of his bedroom had gray dots that looked like mold and water damage. He had a desk, but one of the legs was being propped up by books, and the back of his desk chair had split long ago. His bookshelf was packed, but most of the books were library books that had DISCARD across the spine in big red letters. Even the sheets on his bed, though clean, were threadbare. The only thing that looked new were his clothes, which made sense.

"You guys have gotta believe me. I didn't push Wyn into a hutch because I'm a brute. I pushed Wyn into a hutch because my future depends on it," Judah said firmly. "If you knew what I know, you would have done it, too. This is an evil town, and I want to get my family out of here. Permanently. For people like me and my mom, a chance like this only comes once in a few lifetimes."

"I can't leave here without punching you, or at least doing something," Max said, though I could see that Judah's circumstances were wearing him down. "Unless—do you want to do it, Wyn?"

"By all means," Wyn said, gesturing at Max to do the honors.

"Go ahead. It's the least I deserve," Judah said solemnly.

Max reared his fist back, then stopped. He shook his head, frustrated, and instead he backhanded Judah crisply on the cheek that wasn't shattered.

"For the disrespect."

Judah's face was blazing, but he nodded in agreement, his blond hair falling over his eyes.

"I get you were put into an impossible position, Judah. But you *know* Wyn. She wasn't a stranger to you," I said quietly. "People shouldn't be collateral damage."

Again, I thought about Oly. His charming smile and manic sneer, the histrionic speech he gave before disappearing. Judah and Oly were not the same, but there were currents of this sort of wickedness that seemed to run through many people in this town.

"Did you kill Mr. Wyatt?" I asked him suddenly. His contriteness and desperation were beginning to reframe my understanding of his position in all this.

"Absolutely not." Judah's head snapped up with offense, his blue eyes bright and resolute. "I'll admit I was poking around upstairs looking for the spyglass while everyone was distracted by the cake. But I'm not a murderer."

"Good. I'm trying to stay away from hanging out with murderers. You'd be surprised how difficult that is in this town," I said.

Judah's eyebrows knotted in confusion. "What? No. Look, you seem like a good kid, and I guess that moment in the kitchen did get a bit . . . flirty. But I'm not trying to 'hang out' or whatever. I just wanted to talk to you about my book. Besides, I thought you were dating Wyn?" he asked, looking between the two of us with confusion.

Wyn's cheeks went bright red, and I could feel heat on my own as we pointedly avoided eye contact.

"Oh my god," Max said, mischief quickly replacing the anger in his voice. "That's something I never considered . . . That would be the most interesting non-murdery thing to happen in Hollow Falls in forever."

"Shut up," Wyn and I said at the same time, shooting Max matching scowls.

"We need to focus," I said, eager to change the subject as quickly as possible. "This isn't about me and Wyn—not that there is a me and Wyn. I mean, there is, but it's like—" I waved my arms around semi-hysterically. "We were talking about Judah!"

"And my book," Judah added. "It's like I told you the other night, I've been researching this town my whole life, and I wanted to give you a copy of my magnum opus before I start sending it to literary agents. There's something evil about this place, and you're the only person who might care—or who might be able to do something about it."

Judah went to his desk and pulled open a drawer in the file cabinet underneath which was packed with tabbed folders.

"I'm not a conspiracy theorist or into the supernatural or anything like that. But too many creepy things have happened here, and it was driving me mad that no one ever talks about it," he said, snatching up a file folder and handing it to me. "Everyone acts like everything is an isolated incident or an accident or a tragedy, and it's weird that no one has gathered all these occurrences in one place."

"What's this?" I said, opening the folder and shifting through the papers.

"Those are clippings just from the year before the Lit Killer started his crime spree," Judah said, crossing his arms. "I've been working on this long before that whole mess came to a head."

Max peered over my shoulder and picked a newspaper article out of the folder.

"You would think that the Lit Killer got so much attention because he was a literal serial killer. But the first year he was active wasn't even the most violent year of that decade in Hollow Falls. Most of the deaths are filed as accidental, but what are the odds of so many freak accidents happening in the same town? The year documented in the folder I just gave you had twelve people die from mysterious circumstances alone."

"Is that really that weird? This is a whole town," Max said, frowning.

"We only have six thousand people!" Judah exclaimed. "One of those people went into the grocery store and just vanished into thin air. Another seems to have died from spontaneous combustion—just went up in flames in her living room chair. Nothing else touched in the entire apartment!"

"And the police aren't looking into any of this?" I said suspiciously.

Judah pressed his lips into an angry thin line. "Most of these aren't people of any particular influence. We don't have a big fancy police department or a forensics unit, Tig. If it looks like an accident, it goes down on paper that it was an accident. No one wants to rock the boat or upset any families. The Lit Killer and other sensationalized crimes mostly got attention because there was no mistaking what happened to them. Which begs the question of whether the Lit Killer targeted Hollow Falls specifically? Or did something about the town draw him here?

"That's why I wanted to meet with you. If there is going to be another Hollow Falls Violent Disaster, you should know about the pattern because I won't be around for it."

"Because you're going to college," Max repeated.

"Because I'm going to college," Judah said resolutely. "I'll email you a copy of the manuscript. No pressure to read it or anything; I just want you to have it."

I gave him my email.

"I know I shouldn't ask this, but are you planning to tell the police what happened the other night?" Judah asked quietly.

Max rolled his eyes and walked out of the room without answering, clearly finished with Judah entirely. Wyn shot Judah her own dirty look and trailed after Max.

"No, we're not," I said. "We were breaking and entering, too, you know. But we are going to find out who's responsible for all this. You're right about one thing: This town does have a dark history and a violent past. What's going on is bigger than some spyglass. And we're going to put an end to it."

I followed Max out of the room, leaving Judah sitting dejectedly at his desk, his head in his hands. He was pitiable in some ways, but he was another dead end we didn't have time for.

More than that, I couldn't believe that there had been a time when I almost let myself be intrigued by the thought that he had some interest in me. The idea that I could have found myself with yet another boy capable of violence chilled me a bit. Not to mention that Oly was still out there somewhere, doing god knows what. Definitely nothing good . . .

When I got outside, Max and Wyn were already standing outside Judah's house. Wyn was doing her best to calm Max down, but his arms were crossed and his face tight; he clearly still wasn't in the best of moods.

"What next?" he said snappily.

"This all comes back to the Murder of Crows. Thanks to Noel, we know that she, Abuela, Mr. Green, and Mr. Wyatt worked together on The Hunt until Mr. Wyatt had it all shut down in the '70s. And now, almost fifty years later, Mr. Wyatt's dead and someone blackmailed Judah so they could get their hands on a spyglass that Mr. Wyatt was keeping hidden.

"My gut tells me someone in the Murder of Crows is responsible for this, so we need to talk to someone who broke rank—someone who left The Hunt and everyone involved in it behind.

"It's time for me to talk to Abuela."

Chapter 14

Wyn and Max had offered to go home with me, but I knew I had to talk to Abuela on my own. By the time I got there, the sun had long since slipped away, and the wind was beginning to pick up. My stomach growled. I hadn't eaten since the shared plate of fries at the diner earlier that day. Hopefully my argument with Abuela at the funeral hadn't stopped her from saving me some leftovers.

I could see from the street as I approached that the lights in our house were all off. But when I got to the front door, I found it ajar—and the wooden frame was splintered, as if someone had entered by force.

I took a breath and slipped inside. Instantly I knew I wasn't alone.

I eased down the dark hallway as quietly as possible. As I

got deeper into the house, I noticed a faint light coming from Abuela's room. But it wasn't the steady, warm glow of her bedside lamp. It was a bright, swinging beam—a flashlight being waved around by someone who wasn't supposed to be there.

Peeking around the corner toward her doorway, I was confronted with the broad back of another assailant in black. It wasn't Judah. We had just left his house, and this figure was too tall and too broad, a little more muscular—and he was using that muscle to tear Abuela's bedroom apart.

From the hallway, I could see into my own bedroom, which was similarly ransacked. The hollow book, which I had placed carefully on my bookshelf, was lying open on my bed. The spine was broken, and the hollow cavity inside gaped open. He was looking for the spyglass, then. Why wasn't I surprised?

I turned back to see the intruder prying at the underside of Abuela's dresser drawers with a knife, trying to see if anything had been hidden in the bottom. And then I got a glimpse behind him, and my heart dropped into my stomach.

Lying on the bed, her wrists and ankles tied tight with rope, was my abuela. A piece of duct tape was slapped across her face, and a trail of blood was dripping wetly from her hairline. Her eyes were shining with tears, and when she caught my gaze, she shook her head furiously, trying to warn me away.

Suddenly, I was angrier than I was afraid. I wasn't going to let anyone else get hurt because of me.

"If you're looking for the spyglass, you're not going to find it there," I said lowly.

The man's head snapped up and turned toward me. He flipped the knife deftly in his hand and crouched like he was preparing for a fight.

"I know you need it to find the treasure. And I know you killed Mr. Wyatt to try and get it." My eyes locked with his. "We're not just going to hand it over."

He flipped the knife in his hand again as if considering his next move, then sheathed and pocketed the blade. I relaxed for a second, glad that the sharp steel was no longer in action, but that was time enough for him to lunge forward with incredible speed and grab me by the front of my hair. I screamed in pain and punched him in the chest. This man was clearly more of a professional than Judah because he just grunted and slammed the side of my head violently against the wall.

My teeth rattled in my skull from the blow, and I immediately felt nauseous. I could hear Abuela's muffled screams from behind us. I kicked out at him, making contact with his inner thigh and then kneeing him in the stomach. He absorbed my blows like rocks glancing off a tank, using my hair and compromised balance to fling me into the mess that was my room. I tripped over the lamp, which was on the floor, and stumbled onto the bed. The man pressed himself against me, using the weight of his own body to pin me down as he patted all over, clearly searching.

"Get off!" I screamed.

As I flailed, my backpack slipped from my shoulder and landed on the floor with a loud metallic thunk.

The man's head whipped around at the noise. He bent to grab the bag, rifled inside, and pulled out the spyglass. With a satisfied hum, he pocketed the device. Then he grabbed me by the throat and squeezed until dots swam before my eyes. When he let go, the rush of air spun my head and blackened my vision.

As I lay on the bed, struggling to breathe, I heard more commotion from the hallway. The sound of the thief's footsteps pounded in my aching head, and I heard Abuela's muffled shouts getting quieter and quieter, until they finally disappeared.

By the time I was able to struggle to my feet, vertigo slammed into me like a wave, and I had to pause to steady myself against the dresser. When I finally got my equilibrium back, the house was empty.

I leaned against the door and looked around at the cyclone the thief had left in his wake, before making my way to Abuela's room.

"Abuela?" I cried. But there was no answer. I knew in my gut that there wouldn't be. The bed was empty, the sheets pulled to the ground, like she had clung to them for as long as she could before the intruder had dragged her away. I slid down to the ground and closed my eyes.

My heart was pounding in my ears, and I felt both incandescently furious and so weak with worry I was about to collapse. I went to push myself to my feet, but when I did, my palm slipped on something metal and I fell back, banging my elbow hard.

"What the hell was—" I looked closer. There was a metal chain poking out from between the box spring and the mattress, like someone had shoved it there in a panic but didn't quite have enough time to make sure it was well hidden.

I pulled the chain, and a simple gold piece with a clear circular pendant at the end popped out. It was Abuela's necklace. I had never seen her without it, even when I was a kid. She used it as a magnifying glass to read and sometimes to start bonfires in the summer. It was such a part of her that I knew she'd never leave it behind. Not unless she was forced to. But then why was it hidden?

Suddenly, I remembered something Noel had said. Could Abuela have hidden this for me to find? Was it a clue? Could this help me find her *and* the treasure?

I held the necklace up and draped it around my own neck, holding it close against my heart.

"I think . . ." I said out loud, "it's time to call the police."

And then everything went black.

You would think having the last words you say to someone you love be "I'm sorry" would be a good thing. Very cathartic. But despite what every sappy TV romance says, it really wasn't.

I just kept running through my fight with Abuela at the funeral over and over again, like a nightmare.

When I came to and called 911, I was stuck with the EMTs for what felt like hours as they checked out my head and the bruising on my throat. (Side note: if you've never been punched in the head . . . I would not recommend it.)

And then I had to deal with the cops. If you've listened to the podcast before, you won't be surprised to hear that the Hollow Falls Police Department was no help at all. I shouldn't have expected them to treat me well, especially after the Lit Killer fiasco, but I did hope that they would be a little kind . . . a little sympathetic considering everything I'd just gone through. But no.

Instead, I spent four hours being grilled about Abuela's disappearance and what the thief had taken. Which I couldn't answer without getting into the whole thing about Mr. Wyatt, and I did *not* have time for that. Leave it to Hollow Falls's finest to waste time in a spectacularly ridiculous way by talking to me when they could have been, I don't know, *looking for my abuela*.

By the time I managed to get out of the police station to call my dad, he was back on shift at the oil tanker. I managed to reach his ship, but I couldn't understand a word through the thick Ukrainian accent of whoever picked up the satellite phone. The guy seemed incredibly kind, but I had no idea if he would relay the message in a way that would keep my dad from going ballistic.

I just felt so . . . alone and stressed out, and my head kept pounding painfully. I couldn't go home to a dark, ransacked house.

I just kept thinking . . . what if?

What if I had been there when the intruder arrived?

What if I hadn't been with Judah?

What if Judah had known about the intrusion and kept us there as long as he could with his sob stories so his boss could get away with everything?

What if I never got to see Abuela again and apologize to her the way she deserved?

What if she's not missing?

What if she's not missing.

What if she's actually really gone and I never got to say goodbye?

What if it's all my fault?

Chapter 15

By the time I left the police station, the sky was pink and the chill of the night air was beginning to burn away. I couldn't bear to be alone, so I headed to the Star Diner for a very early breakfast.

When I arrived, the diner was virtually empty, which was a small mercy. There were just a few early risers and Phil, the owner, milling around, brewing coffee, and wiping down tables.

I sat myself at a booth in the back and texted our group chat to tell them where I was. In the spur of the moment, I included Ella, too. She seemed to know more about the Murder of Crows than anybody, and right now, I could use all the help I could get.

The smell of diner food, a favorite of mine, was thick and

cloying, but even rich maple syrup couldn't get my mind off what happened.

Every time I closed my eyes, I could see the intruder's steely gaze, merciless and violent. I could still feel his hands on my skin and hear my abuela's cries.

Phil eventually swung by my table quickly. "You want a coffee, kiddo?"

"NO!" I said much louder than was probably appropriate. "I mean . . . no thank you. Can I just have a few waters for the table?"

"A few waters coming up. Just let me run it through some coffee grounds first. You look like you need it."

Wyn, Max, and Ella pushed their way past the jingling door less than fifteen minutes later and made their way to my table.

"Hey, Tig."

"Hey!" I tried to smile, but I could feel my eyes filling with tears at the sight of my friends.

Wyn's own eyes widened as she took in my bruised neck and the stricken expression on my face. She looked almost sick with concern. "What the hell happened? Are you okay?" She slid in next to me and cupped her hand on my chin, as if to examine my injuries.

Max slid into the opposite side with Ella they all stared at me, waiting for my explanation.

Just then, Phil appeared and thunked four mugs of watery coffee on the table.

"Anything else?" he asked, stifling a yawn.

"Nothing for me," I said quickly.

Max ordered donuts for the table ("You need to eat, Tig"). Ella asked for Splenda, but when the diner's owner simply answered her with a raised eyebrow, she rolled her eyes and requested orange juice instead. We waited until Phil was out of earshot before I gave them a rundown of the last eight hours, from when I got home last night to my encounter with the police.

I shook my head as I finished my recap. "It all happened so fast. I came inside, he was there ransacking the place, and Abuela was all tied up. Before I knew it, I was on the ground and Abuela and the spyglass were gone."

"You're lucky he didn't kill you, Tig," Wyn said. "Thank god for that."

"At least there's one piece of good news," Ella chimed in.

I scoffed. "And what's that?"

"If he was planning to kill your abuela, he wouldn't have bothered taking her with him."

Ella's good news wasn't as reassuring as she thought. That also meant that the intruder must need something from Abuela—something he thought only she could tell him. I raised my hand to Abuela's pendant, now hanging around my neck, and rubbed it softly. I had to figure out what she knew before her kidnapper ran out of patience and decided to find the treasure some other way.

"Do you think it was Judah?" Max said seriously.

"No." I sighed. "He wouldn't have had time to beat me home after we left his house. I guess he could have been stalling us to give whoever it was time to search my house, but . . . I don't think he had anything to do with this.

"The guy who broke in was a pro. I managed to get a few hits in, but he barely made a sound even when the blows landed. And he was so methodical. He didn't even hesitate to . . ." I raised my hand to the side of my head unconsciously.

Max folded his arms. "That's just great! So we have two psychopaths in town willing to beat up teenage girls," he said with a growl.

"Do we think whoever attacked Tig and kidnapped Abuela is the same person who killed Mr. Wyatt? Or are there two separate groups after the spyglass?" Wyn asked, absentmindedly picking the sprinkles off a donut.

"The timeline is way too close for all these incidents not to be unconnected," I said. "My guess is that it's all one person—or a group of people working together. They tried to get the spyglass from Mr. Wyatt, but he wouldn't give it up, so they killed him. And they've been escalating ever since, trying to find it.

"They were probably at the funeral, too," I added. "They could have heard me and Abuela arguing and figured out that we knew about The Hunt. If I had only kept my mouth shut, maybe Abuela would be home safe right now."

I slammed my fist against the table, and Wyn threw an arm around my shoulders. "Stop it, Tig. You can't blame yourself. For all you know, whoever did this could have been someone who was involved in The Hunt originally."

"Yeah," Ella chimed in. "Didn't Noel tell you there were four of them working together? Kind of suspicious that there's only two of them left . . ."

My head shot up. "You're right. Noel said they split up the artifacts needed to find the treasure among themselves. Mr. Wyatt had the spyglass, and our killer got his hands on that, thanks to me. And Mr. Green is supposed to have the original map drawn by the creators of The Hunt."

For some reason, I wasn't ready to tell my friends my theory about Abuela's necklace—not yet.

"So we need to talk to Mr. Green," Max said.

Ella perked up. "Makes sense. I mean, he is the one who dragged you into all this in the first place."

"Exactly. Either he's involved in this and he was gathering

up the missing pieces . . . or whoever's behind this is going to be after him next."

"It's not like we have anything to lose," Wyn said.

I started scooting toward the outside of the booth, but Wyn put a hand on my arm to stop me.

"We don't have to go this second, though. I know you're worried about your abuela—we all are"—Wyn barreled on, anticipating my objections—"but you're not going to be able to help her like this. You need to rest. We can regroup in a few hours."

I looked across the booth at Max and Ella, who were giving me identical looks of concern.

"Fine," I sighed, recognizing defeat. "I'll crash for a couple hours. But then we're going to talk to Mr. Green."

Going to sleep in a big empty house while my abuela was out there somewhere in danger was the worst thing I could think of. Luckily, Wyn agreed to come home with me. If only to make sure I actually got some sleep and didn't just pace around worrying until it was time for us to meet up again.

The closer we got to my house, the more my heart began to race. Wyn took my keys from my trembling hands and unlocked the door. (Not that it mattered with the doorframe busted. But a habit is a habit.)

It was like a role reversal of the night Wyn had been injured. She led me to my room (closing the door to Abuela's room wordlessly as we passed) and swept everything from my bed save the blankets. The last thing I felt before succumbing to sleep was Wyn's hand running gently through my hair.

Chapter 16

By the time I woke up, it was late afternoon, and Wyn refused to apologize for letting me sleep all day. (And although I hated to admit it, I did feel a little bit better after some shut-eye.)

After refueling on the cold leftovers we found in the fridge, Wyn and I planned to meet up with Max at Mr. Green's house, the large Victorian near the bus stop where I'd first met him. I didn't plan to call ahead. I needed to catch him off guard if we were going to get any real information out of him.

When we arrived, I pounded on the door repeatedly until it finally swung open. Mr. Green was wearing another hideous wool suit (a drab brown this time), but he looked much older than he had when I'd seen him last. Even his mustache appeared to be drooping. And despite our showing up unannounced, Mr. Green didn't seem that surprised to see us.

"Ah," he said. "I was wondering when you'd show up."

Mr. Green opened the door wide and gestured for us to enter. His house was modest in comparison to Mr. Wyatt's, and the interior was art deco–inspired, with rich velvet, dark wood, clean lines, and gold furnishings. It was the kind of house where you knew immediately that there was a library inside it somewhere.

Mr. Green sat us down with him in his sunroom so that we could watch the birds in his garden. Then he doled out small cakes and cookies and delicate cups and saucers filled with a floral-smelling tea.

"Are you done stalling?" I asked sharply once he settled into his own chair.

Mr. Green sighed. "Alan asked you to find the founder's treasure, didn't he?"

"Yeah," Wyn responded. "And since then we've witnessed a man fall to his death, Tig and I have both been attacked, and Mrs. Torres has been kidnapped!"

Mr. Green gasped and nearly dropped his saucer. "Sofia has been kidnapped?" He looked to me as if for confirmation. I nodded sharply, the lump in my throat making it difficult to speak.

"When Alan told me he thought things were ramping up

again, I told him he was being silly. I never thought . . . For fifty years, there haven't been more than whispers about The Hunt. I thought we had effectively wiped it from living memory."

"Your book-burning campaign was a success," Max chimed in. "We could barely find anything about The Hunt in the library. You missed the *Talon* archives, though." He grinned, and Mr. Green managed a weak chuckle.

"Bookish people like you, my young detective, are hobbled at the knees without their research. Reduced to interviews and old-fashioned guesswork. The purest of all capers . . . the most prestige of cases lying in your lap."

"When Mr. Wyatt said they removed all references to the founder's treasure from public record, I didn't think he really meant it quite so literally."

Mr. Green took a sip of his tea.

"You should always fight for the preservation of knowledge," he said sagely. "So much is lost if it is destroyed forever. Alan allowed me to keep a few books on subjects I admire, and he had one version of every edition we removed in his library, but there was so much richness that was burned in order to protect the people of Hollow Falls."

"How did that work out for you?" Wyn asked.

Mr. Green fixed me with a steely gaze. "The only places

information on the founder's treasure can be found are in people. People are a kind of book, you know. The original book: storytellers."

He put his teacup down and folded his hands in his lap. "The main issue is that we are delicate . . . impermanent. Not the most infallible keepers of information. There are things only Alan, Noel, Sofia, and I know. We thought that by splitting up the artifacts and agreeing to keep them apart—to keep ourselves apart, to an extent—we could contain The Hunt and prevent people from pursuing it. But I suppose greed is the greatest of motivators."

He paused for a long moment. "And you consider me a suspect, am I right?"

"If you're involved in all this, you're not doing it alone," I said, maintaining eye contact with Mr. Green. "Not to be rude, but you're not strong enough to carry Abuela anywhere against her will. And you were literally downstairs serving cake when Mr. Wyatt fell. So unless you have teleportation powers, it had to be someone else."

Mr. Green huffed in amusement. "Very true."

"Uh, shouldn't you be more upset about your best friend's murder—not to mention being accused of committing it?" Max asked.

Mr. Green shook his head. "We lived our youth flirting

with danger. We never expected to get this old at all—Sofia included. The golden summer had our nails ringed with blood and our adrenaline pumping day in and day out. Alan went out in a blaze of glory, not lying sick in bed. As long as whoever did this to him gets their just deserts, I'll choose to celebrate his life rather than mourn his death," he said wistfully. "In fact, Wyatt is probably looking up at us from hell right now, raging at me to start swinging a club around to avenge him."

"Hell?" I said, scandalized.

"Heaven wouldn't be interesting enough for him," he said firmly.

"Can you tell us what happened between you all?" I practically begged. "I can't help thinking that if I know more about Abuela when she was younger, it will help me figure out what's going on and how to find her."

Mr. Green looked wistful. "Alan and I were always neck and neck with Sofia and Noel in pursuit of the founder's treasure. They would beat us to one location, and we'd beat them to the next. We didn't officially meet until the night a man named Jet Cassidy died. He was—"

"The librarian who died in the church," I interjected.

"Yes," Mr. Green said, sounding surprised. "That really was the beginning of the end. We spent another couple months working together, trying to piece together the last few clues and discover the location of the treasure. But the fighting became too much. Alan didn't want to see someone else die the way Jet had. We decided collectively that it would be better if the treasure was never found.

"Would you like to hear the story of what happened that night—the night I met your grandmother?"

We all nodded, and Mr. Green settled back into his chair and began to speak.

"I can't believe he beat us here!" Sofia said, shaking her long dark curls angrily.

Noel took a long drag on her cigar as Sofia tucked her machete back in its sheath.

"I'm just glad we don't have to fight him," she said, breathing smoke out into the chill air. "Although I bet he wished he'd minded his business. Your blade would have hurt a lot less than that."

Jet Cassidy, the local librarian (and riddle thief), lay mangled at their feet from his hideous fall. The blood was still rolling down the main aisle to the front door of the church.

Sofia wrinkled her nose. "Come, Noel, don't be cruel.

A man just died—even if it is his own damn fault."

Noel stretched and rolled her shoulders. She shifted the wheel of rope she had brought from one side to the other.

"Well. What do you wanna do now, darlin'?" she asked. "The fellas from the club must be on our tail. Or do you think they saw the body and bailed? You can always count on a man to have a weak stomach."

Sofia peered into the night suspiciously. "The blood's too fresh. Mr. Cassidy couldn't have fallen more than ten, fifteen minutes ago. I think we beat the Murder of Crows for once."

Sofia leaned down to examine the body as closely as possible, without disrupting the scene. "He doesn't seem to be holding anything, so what we're looking for might still be up there. I think we should take our chances . . . but if we do, we have to do it now. There's no time to waste."

Sofia rolled up her pant legs, tucked in the laces of her shoes, and hopped her way across the church floor, avoiding the splashes of blood. Noel leaned down and put out her cigar on the stone floor of the church and then came up close behind her companion, following her to the staircase leading to the balcony.

The girls thundered up the steps. "We've gotta be close after this one, right? How many could be left?" Sofia asked.

"How about none?" a voice from the landing echoed. "Get out of the church. This one's ours."

Sofia looked up to see two shadows silhouetted by the light of the moon. The Murder of Crows had made it to this location after all. The two men wore masks and gloves so you couldn't see their eyes or hands. One of them—the taller of the two—was holding a rapier and the other had a common billy club. Sofia didn't know which was more dangerous.

"We're getting whatever's up there. Get out of our way before someone else has to die tonight," Sofia warned.

The Crows switched places, the larger one in front and the shorter, more slender one in the back. They had silently decided who would be fighting who.

"Fine," Noel snapped.

She threw her rope like a lasso around one of the men's necks. Clearly very well trained, he stuck his club underneath at the last moment, wrenching it upward to free himself before Noel could tighten it.

The larger man advanced on Sofia and swung his rapier in a wild arc. Sofia blocked it easily with her machete, but he used the connection of their blades to push her backward down the stairs. She stumbled but caught her balance. Sofia couldn't see this man's face, but she could swear he was grinning.

He rushed forward with powerful strikes, his only weakness, the flexibility of his blade. The machete Sofia carried was shorter, stronger, and much sturdier. But it also shortened her reach and put her in more danger. She took a precious second to glance behind her and hopped back down five stairs, rolling to her feet. The man froze and looked back up the stairs for a moment.

Sofia could hear Noel holding her own, the sound of a large weight hitting the floor punctuated by a cry that was certainly not hers. Sofia smiled.

"Where did you learn to fight?"

The man sliced across the air, and Sofia ducked just in time, the blade slicing the tips of her hair as it floated behind her.

"Wouldn't you like to find out?" she teased, jumping up on a pew to avoid stepping in gore and leaving her footprints behind.

The man didn't take the bait, but he saw what his opponent was doing and followed suit, standing on a pew behind her. Their blades sung and clashed as they fought, slipping down the polished wood. Suddenly, Sofia stumbled, dropping her blade as her foot collided with a hymnal someone had left on the bench in the dark.

She screamed, but before her head could crash against the edge of the pew, the man reached out quick as a flash and snagged the front of her sweater tight in his grip.

Sofia panted in surprise as he hauled her back up. She pressed her hands against his chest and stared into the black void of his mask.

The man gently let her down and without a word clapped her in handcuffs. "Try beating us to the treasure now," he said with glee.

Sofia looked down at the clink of the metal. "Hey!"

"Sofia!" Noel shrieked from above.

Sofia and her opponent looked up. Noel's rope was wrapped around the base of the chandelier. She was holding on to the other end with an iron grip, shimmying her way up the rope toward the fixture. The Murder of Crows member who had chased after her was nowhere to be seen.

"It's not steady," the taller man shouted from his place beside Sofia. "Get down from there!"

"I'm so close," Noel said. "I can see something glittering."

A thrum of terror ran through Sofia as she saw her dearest friend dangling from the ceiling.

"Get down, Noel! We can find another way!" she shouted.

There was a horrible creaking sound. The chandelier tinkled dangerously. Noel's opponent wobbled into view. He had chased her up the final set of stairs, and he was now holding his head in his hands, like he'd just regained consciousness. The instant his eyes focused on Noel, he, too, began shouting.

"What are you doing? A man literally died doing this tonight!" he yelled, gesturing to Jet's broken body.

"I've almost got it . . ." Noel said.

The chandelier let out another metallic whine, and Sofia screeched in terror.

"Noel, I'll never forgive you if you don't get down from there. The treasure isn't worth it! I cannot lose you—not like this!" Sofia yelled.

But Noel didn't listen. She edged her body even closer to the chandelier, and her fingers closed over something tightly.

"Whew! Got it," she crowed triumphantly. "You gotta have a little faith, baby! Two for the clue crew!"

"I'm not kidding!" the man on the balcony said hysterically. He reached out his arms to try to guide her back to solid ground—their differences forgotten in the face of actual danger.

Noel sighed heavily and scooted back down the rope, but that bit of movement was too much for the chandelier to take. It began tearing from the ceiling with a horrible crunch, leaving one side still embedded in plaster—for now. The rope, which had been pulled taut against the base of the chandelier, began to slip, and Noel finally screamed.

"Noel! Noel!" Sofia cried, dashing across the pews to stand directly beneath Noel to break her fall, but her hands were still cuffed together.

"Uncuff me!" she shrieked.

The taller man darted forward, and with a flash of his key, Sofia was free. She turned toward the staircase.

"We don't have time!" her opponent cried. "Cut her rope, and I'll catch her."

Sofia looked up at her friend dangling from the ceiling, and then to the man beside her whom she'd been fighting mere moments before. She hesitated.

"Trust me," he urged. And for some reason, she did.

The chandelier let out another horrifying sound. Sofia snatched up her machete. She moved back to a better angle, took a deep breath, and threw her machete like a tomahawk up at the ceiling. It pinwheeled through the air, glinting dangerously in the moonlight before snapping right through the rope that held Noel up and burying itself in the staircase at the far end of the church.

Noel fell screaming toward the granite. The taller man held out his large muscular arms and lowered himself into a crouch, planting his feet firmly on the ground. Noel landed in his arms. He let out a pained grunt and lowered them both to the floor, cushioning some of Noel's momentum from the drop, but his knee still made a horrible cracking sound.

Noel scrambled out of his grip and ran toward Sofia.

"I got it!" She held out a brass spyglass.

But she barely made it two steps before the hardware holding the chandelier up—already tested by Jet earlier in the night, and then again by Noel—finally gave out. With a groan, the heavy glass fixture tore from the plaster and plummeted to the stone below.

Noel dove for Sofia, who dragged her across the aisle, and their opponent managed to roll on his mangled knee in the other direction.

When the dust settled, the ground was littered with so much pulverized glass it looked like the inside of a snow globe.

Sofia held on to Noel tightly for a moment in the aftermath, and then she pushed her away just as suddenly.

"How could you?!" she cried. "This was supposed to be our adventure. It can't be ours if you're dead!"

"A girl had to try, didn't she? I mean, we've come all this way."

"You wouldn't have gone any further if he hadn't been there to catch you!" Sofia gestured wildly at the man before realizing that she didn't actually know his name.

He must have seen the question on her face. "Alan Wyatt," he said with a groan as his partner scrambled down the stairs and rushed to his side, pulling Alan's arm over his shoulder to help bear some of the injured man's weight. "And this is Charles Green."

"A pleasure," Sofia responded, before quickly introducing herself and Noel.

Noel and Sofia had a brief and silent conversation—the way that only the closest of friends can—and Noel finally relented.

"So, fellas, do you want to help us find a treasure?"

Chapter 17

Mr. Green finished his story and took a long drink of his tea before putting the cup back down in the saucer resolutely.

I rubbed the side of my head. "That's . . . honestly a lot to take in. A machete?"

Mr. Green smirked, the wrinkles on the sides of his eyes crinkling delightfully. "She's good with it, too," he said.

"I'm more focused on Noel smoking cigars and slinging a lasso," Wyn said. "What a badass."

Mr. Green chuckled. "Yes, yes, they were spitfires. Still are, I bet. Although before yesterday, I hadn't spoken to Sofia for a long time . . ."

"What happened next?" Wyn asked eagerly.

Mr. Green sighed. "The four of us spent the rest of the

summer working together, trying to crack the last few riddles and to figure out how the spyglass worked with the old map Alan and I had found previously. But we realized soon thereafter that there was a piece missing from the spyglass—the lens. It could have fallen out in the commotion of Noel's fall, or it could have been missing for decades before that. I searched the church high and low after they removed Jet's body, but I didn't find anything. We never figured out what happened to it."

I cleared my throat awkwardly, and Wyn shot me a look.

"Is the missing lens what drove you all apart? Noel mentioned that Jet's death seemed to be a tipping point for The Hunt."

"I suppose you could say that," Mr. Green said. "I can't say for certain how Noel and Sofia were together before that night, but afterward, they were prone to arguing. Sofia never seemed to forgive Noel for risking her life for that spyglass. Sofia didn't think The Hunt was worth all that, and I have to say that Alan and I agreed. His knee was never the same after that night, either.

"Noel wanted to continue on—the risks be damned—but without our cooperation and without the spyglass and the map, she couldn't. She joined the Murder of Crows to stay close to the history of The Hunt, and we remained friendly, of course. But I do think she resented how it all played out, and resented us for our part in taking the treasure from her."

"And my abuela?" I asked softly.

Mr. Green looked at me kindly. "I think she took the loss of her friend harder than we could have imagined. Noel chose The Hunt over their relationship—something I think she regretted, by the way—and I expect it was simply easier to pretend the whole thing had never happened.

"As you get older, your understanding of certain tragedies deepens. You learn what could have been, and it turns things that were funny or adventurous into things that make you sad or angry. Sofia had a lot of adventure in her back then. But it dimmed the night at the church fifty years ago. We all handle grief differently, you see . . ."

A pang shot through my chest. All this time, and my abuela had been suffering in silence. I wished she had told me. I had to find her to give her the chance.

"So that's when you rebranded The Hunt into Founder's Day?" Wyn asked, slipping into her *Talon* reporter voice.

"The mayor was all too happy to help end the deaths and property damage caused by The Hunt. His offices arranged for the new, while Alan and I organized the erasing of the old. We spent ages pulping books, burning maps, and purging libraries, the schools, and even people's homes."

He leaned in conspiratorially. "We exchanged old books about the town for new 'updated' ones for free, and nearly everyone took them. The ones who refused, well. I'll just say, hypothetically, they were burglarized in the night."

"Jeez," Max said.

Mr. Green raised an eyebrow and took another sip of his tea. "Anyway, after everything was destroyed, Alan and I agreed to take possession of the artifacts we had found and to never share with the other where we had hidden them. That way, we could prevent the treasure from ever falling into the wrong hands. Without the map, one would never be able to solve the riddles, and without the spyglass, one could never read the map."

"Can we see the map—please?" I begged. "It might be the only way we can find my abuela. If we can offer it to her kidnapper in exchange—"

"As much as I wish I could help," Mr. Green interrupted me, "I am embarrassed to say that I did not hold up my end of the bargain. The map disappeared from its hiding place over twenty years ago, and I was too ashamed to ever tell Alan the truth."

I gaped at him. I could feel my hope of finding Abuela slipping through my fingers.

"Do you have any idea what happened to it?" Max asked.

"I've always suspected Noel had it. She told Sofia, Alan, and me that she was done looking for the treasure after our falling-out. But when Franklin joined the Murder of Crows, it shifted something in her. I wouldn't put it past her to betray our trust by stealing the map back."

"Franklin Baker?" Wyn asked, tilting her head to the side thoughtfully. "That jerk who came to get us from the library?"

"He was a horrible child who grew into a distasteful adult. But Noel is fond of him; she's fond of all brilliant people. They've been passively searching for the treasure together for close to a decade."

"If that's the case, why is all of this happening now?" I asked.

Mr. Green picked up his teacup and saucer. "When Levinson began to kill again after all these years, I believe they panicked. Years of hunting makes it hard to imagine that everyone isn't after what you're searching for. Levinson wasn't looking for treasure—he was looking for blood. But their paranoia was enough to rekindle the desperation. And to think we've come to this."

I shook my head in disgust as Wyn and Max also got to their feet, sensing this visit was about to come to an end.

"Thank you for your time, Mr. Green. You've been

incredibly helpful," I said. "But it looks like we owe Noel another visit."

"A man my age is no stranger to losing friends, but I'm not anxious to do it again so quickly," he said quietly before we reached the doorway. "I truly hope you find Sofia."

"Trust me, we will."

Chapter 18

"That was super informative and very cool, but also a bit messed up," Wyn said. "I wasn't really that suspicious of Noel when we talked to her before, but I'm definitely feeling it now."

The street darkened as we passed beneath a dense group of trees. It wasn't quite night yet, but the sky was purple and gloomy.

"So do we think she and Franklin are working together to find the treasure?" Max asked. "Why would they have taken Abuela, though, if they already had the map and the spyglass?"

"Because of this," I said. I fingered the necklace around my neck, then took a deep breath and lifted it up from its hiding place beneath my shirt so everyone could see.

My friends gasped.

"Is that . . . the missing lens?" Wyn asked reverently.

I nodded and stroked the lens softly with the pad of my thumb. "Abuela's worn this necklace every day for as long as I've known her. My theory is that she found the broken piece of the spyglass that day in the church and pocketed it, suspecting that things might go south with The Hunt. She probably thought that by stopping her friends from using the spyglass to read the map, she was protecting them."

"And she went all these years without telling anyone?" Max asked. "Your abuela has gotten infinitely cooler in the last hour."

"But someone must have figured it out, right?" Wyn asked.

But before I could answer, my phone rang. I pulled it out of my pocket and, just for a moment, let myself believe it was my abuela calling, safe and sound back at home.

Not quite.

"It's Noel," I muttered to my friends before hitting accept and putting the phone on speaker. "Noel?"

"Tig!" she said hysterically. "Thank god you answered. I think I know where Sofia is!"

"That would make sense considering you helped kidnap her!" I shouted into the phone.

"I understand why you would think that, and I can explain

everything later. But Franklin has been doing all of this without my knowledge. He betrayed me and has been looking for the treasure on his own.

"He called me not long ago and asked me to bring him the map. He said he finally had all the missing pieces, and we could go collect the treasure together. But I knew if he truly had the missing pieces, that meant he had Sofia. I'm driving over there as fast as I can. You have to meet me. We can end this. His address is 1345 South Whipple Avenue."

Without giving us a chance to respond, Noel ended the call.

"That's a trap, right?" Max asked. "It feels like a trap."

I ran my hand through my tangled curls and exhaled sharply. "I mean, maybe? But it's not like we can *not* go. Either she's leading us to Abuela or she knows where she is. Either way, I'm going. But I totally get it if you guys want to wait for reinforcements."

"We're coming," Wyn said immediately, and Max nodded in agreement.

"Okay, so let's go."

Wyn pulled to the front to lead. "Whipple's not that far," she shouted over her shoulder. "Maybe half a mile."

"Just keep running," Max called behind me.

We tore through the streets at top speed, dodging townspeople taking their dogs for evening walks and skidding sharply at corners. Wyn hit one last turn, nearly tripping on her feet as she slowed to a stop. My throat was thick with tears by the time we arrived. This was ending tonight one way or the other.

Franklin Baker's lawn was a vast meadow of white rocks. Not a single blade of grass on the entire property. Disconcertingly there was no car in Franklin's driveway, but a gray car that couldn't belong to anybody but Noel was partially driven up onto the sidewalk, with the door hanging ominously open.

I had a brief flashback to how it felt to enter Levinson's lair last year, but I pushed through it as I approached the front door.

Franklin's house was ruthlessly modern, a monstrosity of steel and glass as black as Noel's house had been gray, with a sleek, totally solid wooden door—without even a keyhole or a mail slot.

Thankfully the door was cracked open a bit, so we burst inside without knocking. Franklin's house looked just as sterile and cold on the inside as it had on the outside. From the doorway, we could see that his kitchen had black granite floors, black stainless-steel appliances, and a black marble island, directly across from an open-plan living room. There was a ring of chairs low to the ground circling a woodblock coffee table and a large couch with its high back to the front door. Worse, the handle of something metal was sticking up from behind the seating, and there was a shiny, wet puddle spreading across the dark wood floors.

"Abuela!" I screamed.

There was a gurgling wheeze in reply, and my blood went ice cold. I vaulted over Franklin's couch in a single leap and nearly landed on top of Noel.

The older woman was sprawled in the center of Franklin's living room in a dark and rapidly spreading pool of her own blood. She was pinned to the expensive gray rug with a rapier like a butterfly on display.

"Oh my god!" Wyn shouted.

Max automatically went to wrap his hand around the blade.

"DON'T PULL IT OUT!" I yelled, and he backed away immediately. "That sword is the only thing keeping her alive right now."

"I think it's much too late for that, dear," Noel murmured. "I never thought I'd be granted a peaceful death, although I admit I didn't think it would hurt quite this much."

"Where's Abuela?" I demanded. "You said she was here. Where did Franklin take her?"

Noel chuckled, her teeth crimson and gory. "Oh, I wish I still had your energy for adventure." She coughed, speckles of blood flying from between her lips. "I took the founder's map from Mr. Green years ago. I knew I couldn't find the treasure without the spyglass, but I liked knowing that I still had a piece of my youth. That maybe, someday, I could complete what I started all those years ago."

She closed her eyes. I crouched down closer to hear her.

"Franklin knew I had the map, but we hadn't worked closely on The Hunt together in years. He took it all much more seriously, especially after Mr. Levinson. I understand now how Sofia felt dealing with me." She laughed, which set her on another round of coughing, the sound wetter than it had been just moments before. "But when Franklin asked me to bring the map here, he said we could find the treasure together. He had the spyglass. We could go together . . . my life's work.

"When I got here, Sofia was with him. I saw this around her neck at the church"—she reached up and grazed the lens around my neck with her bloody fingers—"I knew she had risked her own life to keep the treasure safe. To keep *me* safe. I couldn't just . . . I couldn't leave her . . ."

Noel took a deep breath and reached up to touch the blade that was ending her life.

"She was better with swords than I ever was. But I tried. You have to believe I tried." She gazed up at me plaintively. "But Franklin is younger and stronger and greedy.

He used the spyglass . . . He took her to the chapel . . ."

Noel wrapped her hand around the blade and without a single warning jerked it out of the ground and slid it through her own chest, then tossed it to the side.

Wyn heaved and turned away from the sight.

"I can't die trapped. I have to die free. I have to—" Noel breathed out a long sigh and lay still.

I climbed to my feet and picked up the sword.

"What do we do now?" Wyn said, wiping her mouth.

I shined the blade against the side of Franklin's couch, destroying it with Noel's lifeblood, then tucked the handle in one of my belt loops.

"We go to the chapel, and we get Abuela back."

Chapter 19

By the time we made it back outside, it was dark and had started to rain.

"Let's take Noel's car," Wyn said, and she slid into the driver's seat of the gray Mercedes left in front of Franklin's house. "I think she'd want us to."

Max and I hopped in and slammed the doors, and Wyn sped up the street, heading north.

"What chapel was she talking about?" I asked.

Max sighed. "It's gotta be the one by the Montague Hotel. Years ago, when the Montague was still a reform school, the nuns who ran the place built the chapel. I learned all about its sordid past when I was researching my *Talon* article."

Wyn turned onto a more rural street and started heading up an incline. "Did you know they still used the chapel for weddings up until the '80s? My parents got married there. Great views. But isn't the hotel still under construction?"

"Yeah, but the chapel isn't on the actual grounds. It's adjacent. The only thing is . . ."

"What?" I said. Max was pausing for too long, and it was spiking my anxiety.

"If my research is anything to go by, the chapel is kind of by the old mines . . . or at least where the mines used to be before they were closed down."

"Awesome," I said sarcastically. "That's exactly where I was hoping we'd go. Into some abandoned mines after a middle-aged man who can't complete a scavenger hunt without killing a bunch of old people."

"He's not killing all of them," Wyn responded, squeezing my hand tightly. "We're going to rescue your abuela and get justice for Mr. Wyatt and Noel."

Max huffed and turned his attention to the road whipping past us outside. "This is so cliché," he mumbled. "A boss fight in the middle of the night in the rain."

We rounded the corner, and the Montague Hotel jutted out before us. Or at least what they had left of it. The construction seemed to be going pretty well. The building was about half completed, still covered with heavy-duty building plastic, which whipped around wildly in the rain. The chapel was maybe one or two city blocks away. Close enough to see with the human eye, far enough for it to be a hell of a march as it poured.

Wyn pulled up as close as she could to the chapel; then she turned off the car, and we dashed up the hill. As we approached, I noticed that the chapel door was open a crack, and a bright beam of light was spilling out into the night.

We all paused when we got to the door, steeling ourselves for what we might find inside. I took a deep breath, stuck my head into the open door, and moaned in relief. Abuela was sitting down on the remainder of one of the chapel's old pews, still tied at the hands and feet. It was a grim parallel to the last time I'd seen her at Mr. Wyatt's funeral, but I'd never been happier to see anyone in my life.

I rushed inside, Wyn and Max fast on my heels, and dropped to my knees in front of Abuela, clutching her legs in a desperate embrace. I noticed Max swinging his head from side to side, examining every inch of the small chapel. The space was lit with a tall construction lamp set up in one corner, but Franklin was nowhere to be found.

I finally stood when I felt Abuela tugging at my elbow with her bound hands. The ropes around her ankles were loose—Franklin must have forced her to walk at least part of the way here. The ones around her wrists, though, were tight, the skin underneath rubbed raw. Franklin had taped her mouth, too, but one edge was loose, and I eased it from her lips slowly. She sighed with relief and grazed my cheek with her knuckles softly.

"You shouldn't have come, mija."

"Yeah, that was never an option," I said, squeezing my abuela's hands tightly. "Where is he?"

She nodded toward the grime-covered window near the back of the chapel. I could just make out a figure roaming in the darkness, the low beam of a flashlight skating across the ground.

"I think he partly took me because he was hoping you would follow. He seemed convinced Mr. Wyatt told you something he doesn't know. Luckily, he seemed to believe me when I said I didn't have another artifact and didn't know how to read the map. But he was sort of stuck with me at that point."

"Not for much longer. We have to hurry."

Max and Wyn crouched down behind the bench and started untying Abuela's legs, while I used the sword to try to saw away at the much-tighter ropes around her hands. She gazed at the rapier with a mixture of sadness, disgust, and relief. If I was remembering Mr. Green's story correctly, it must have belonged to Mr. Wyatt—Franklin's memento from the murder? But it was also stained with Noel's blood. The rope was fraying, but the rapier simply wasn't sharp enough. It was a stabbing sword, not a cutting one, and I was starting to sweat with anxiety.

"I wondered when you would show up!"

I whipped around. Franklin was standing in the shadow of the chapel doors. He was dressed in his intruder outfit, minus the black mask, and he looked comically villainous. His normally well-coifed hair was slicked down with the rain. He entered the chapel and reached out a hand toward us.

"My sword," he demanded.

"It's not yours!" I cried, tucking the blade behind me.

Franklin laughed. "Of course it is. What, did you think it was Alan's? He's not the only person interested in swordplay. How do you think we met? Now give it here."

I didn't move. Franklin rolled his eyes and reached behind him, pulling out a sawed-off shotgun from a holster on his back.

Max and Wyn screamed and Abuela recoiled, but I stayed steady and tightened my grip.

"Let's try again, shall we? Hand me my sword," Franklin said.

"Why do you need it so badly?" I asked.

Franklin looked annoyed for a moment, then seemed to reconsider.

"Fine. Keep the sword for now. It's not like you can do much with it in here," he said, looking around the chapel with a bored expression.

He took a step farther into the small room, and we all stepped back instinctively, shielding Abuela with our own bodies. Franklin chuckled softly to himself and continued walking, stopping at a handsome leather messenger bag sitting on the pew across the aisle. He placed his shotgun on the wooden bench slowly—making eye contact with me as he did so—before turning away from us and digging into the bag. When he finally faced us again, he was holding a large, yellowed piece of paper lined with crease marks.

The map.

"You know, when I used your spyglass to look at Noel's map, it points right to this old chapel as the location of the founder's treasure.

"By the way, thank you for being so accommodating, Tig," Franklin said with a twisted smile. "If only Noel had done the same."

"You coward," Wyn spat.

In a flash, Franklin's shotgun was in his hand again. He flicked off the safety and pointed it at us, the map fluttering slowly to the stone floor at his feet.

"As I was saying. Behind this chapel—which is a holdover from when the Montague Hotel was a convent and reform school, if you can believe it—there is a stack of limestone blocks. Now, supposedly these were part of an old shrine behind the chapel. But if you ask me, they look like they're sealing off something good. It seems like the perfect hiding spot for a centuries-old treasure, no?"

Franklin holstered the shotgun and stepped over the map on his way to the door.

"If you attempt to leave this chapel, I'll hunt you down and end your lives," he said casually. "I've been searching for this treasure for three decades, and I need an audience to witness my victory."

"That's embarrassing," Max whispered.

"*That's embarrassing,*" Franklin mimicked him in a high-pitched voice. "Nothing is more embarrassing than failure. Remember that."

Then he turned to me once more. "The sword."

I hesitated. The chapel had clearly been abandoned for decades. Every inch was coated in dust, anything valuable long since pilfered, and the wooden beams along the ceiling and walls were dangerously bowed. In here, we had nothing but our hands and this blade to protect ourselves or make our escape. Without it, we were as good as dead.

"The sword," he repeated again, one hand reaching back toward his shotgun. I handed it over.

Franklin took the sword with a polite nod and walked off toward the only exit and the raging storm outside.

The doors slammed behind him, the few remaining windows rattling in their panes. Max raced after him, but when he went to jerk the handles, they rattled ominously.

Wyn followed and peered out from the small circular windows in the door. "He chained them shut," she said, her voice shaking.

From outside, we heard a roar—but not thunder. It was the sound of one of the large excavators from the construction site at the hotel. We all watched in shock as Franklin drove past the front doors, straight out into the night, heading for the back of the chapel.

The pile of limestone rocks was directly behind us, less than a hundred yards away, hidden by shadows. I hadn't noticed them on our race to get inside and rescue Abuela, but they were perfectly in sight from the windows on the chapel's far wall.

We watched in silence for a moment as Franklin drove deeper into the darkness, the headlights of the machinery and its low rumble the only signs it was still there. We heard more than saw as he shifted gears and began using the digging machine to lift the limestone blocks away—exposing whatever was lying underneath.

Max folded his arms. "I can't believe he's making us watch this. If anyone is a candidate for therapy, it's him."

"He's probably going to need more than therapy in a moment," Abuela said darkly.

"We have to find something sharp to cut this rope," Wyn said anxiously, gesturing toward Abuela's still-bound wrists. She wandered to the other side of the room and began kicking at the old beer cans and hymnals littering the floor.

"And we need to figure out what to do after he gets the treasure. Because I have a feeling we're only worth keeping alive until then." I bent to pick up the map Franklin had dropped, folded it gently, and stuck it inside the messenger bag. I gave a cursory glance at the rest of its contents, but there was nothing in the bag that would help keep us alive if Franklin got bored.

"He's not getting the treasure," Abuela said resolutely.

Max and I stared at her. "Do you know where the treasure is?" I asked, shocked.

Abuela shrugged. "No, but he doesn't know, either. He has the map and the spyglass, but he doesn't have that." She gestured at the necklace around my neck. "You can't read the final location on the map without the lens. The map uses some sort of invisible ink to show the locations of the riddles. You can see those with the spyglass, but the lens shows you another layer of the ink—almost like 3-D. The only thing at the end of this journey is probably some kind of booby trap."

"What do you mean?" I asked more insistently. Lightning flashed across the sky, and I saw Franklin remove the last of the limestone bricks and begin to dig into the earth below.

"I can't say for sure," Abuela said. "But the creators of the founder's treasure intended for it to be found by a certain kind of person. Someone who tried to skip a step—due to greed or theft—would likely be punished for their mistake. But it's been over a hundred and fifty years. It's possible whatever they left behind is no longer there."

Or maybe it was.

Franklin whooped loudly, then hopped down from the digging machine and disappeared into the darkness beyond it. He emerged from the hole he'd dug with a box in his hands, its outline a dark smudge in the darkness.

Franklin disappeared again, and a minute later, we heard a rattle as the chains around the chapel doors fell to the wet ground with a thud. The doors swung open, and Franklin stood silhouetted in the entryway. Lightning flashed again, illuminating him and the rusted box in his arms.

I could *feel* Max roll his eyes beside me. "What a drama queen," he muttered under his breath.

Franklin finally walked the box over to us and placed it on the floor.

"Perfect!" he cried, ever the narcissist. His eyes were shiny and manic. "Take out your phones. I want photographic evidence that I was the one who found this."

Max grimaced, and Wyn closed the gap between us at a jog, sliding something into her back pocket as she approached.

Thankfully, Franklin didn't seem to notice. He was too busy shoving the sharp end of the rapier into the metal box's seal. He worked it around the perimeter until the corrosion broke off and the only thing keeping it shut was a lock.

Then he stood up and pointed the shotgun at the box, blasting the lock off it in one go. My ears rang from the proximity of the shot as the sound echoed in the stone chapel, and I could feel Abuela go rigid beside me as Franklin opened the lid. A puff of dry air and dust emerged from the box. Inside were a pile of bones and a note.

"What is this?" he said. He lifted the bones up into the air. "WHAT IS THIS?"

"It looks like a pig skeleton," Abuela replied blandly.

Hands shaking, Franklin read the note out loud.

"'Greed without giving, reward without patience, strength without tenderness. Only the foolhardy cease without striving for more than glittering treasure. A life empty and well deserved.'"

"WHAT IS THIS?!" Franklin roared again.

Max took a picture.

Franklin threw the pig skeleton to the side and violently lunged at Max, slapping his phone out of his hand. It cracked against the ground, the screen shattering.

"Hey!" Max cried.

Franklin whirled on Abuela. "YOU. What do you know about this? WHERE IS THE TREASURE?"

Abuela spat at him, and he snarled with rage. "The only thing I know is that you were outsmarted by people who understood your character years before you were ever born," she cried.

Franklin didn't like that at all. He swung his shotgun in an arc, pointing it at us in turn. We all jumped back from him, and he used the opportunity to seize Abuela by her throat.

"I'm going to throw you into the pit and cover it with rocks, and you'll never see the light of day again," he snarled. "How's *that* for a treasure?"

Abuela narrowed her eyes. "But what if the true treasure is still in there? Perhaps you just have to dig deeper."

"We'll see, won't we?" he said primly, and began dragging her forward.

I wrapped my arms around her waist, and Wyn did the same on the other side. Max reached for Franklin's arm, but he turned and smashed Max across the face hard with the butt of his gun. Max stumbled backward, and there was a loud ripping sound as his shirt tore on a jagged piece of wood sticking up from one of the pews.

"Let go of her. Just get your stupid treasure and leave us alone!" Wyn yelled.

Franklin snapped his teeth like a feral animal.

"No, seriously," I said. "What do you have to gain by this? It's literally raining into the hole. It's only going to get harder to keep digging and spot what's inside the muddier it gets."

Abuela smiled. "You wouldn't want to waste your time."

Franklin wasn't a stupid man, and these were great points. He squeezed Abuela's neck tightly, just for the cruelty of it, then let go and marched back toward the doors.

"If there's nothing in there, I'll shoot you all and bury you there," he tossed casually over his shoulder. "Why waste a good hole?"

Franklin pulled the doors closed behind him with a crash, and we heard the chains rattling as he locked them around the handles, sealing us inside for the second time.

Wyn and I rushed to Max's side as soon as Franklin was gone. Max had pulled himself to his feet, but his face was covered in blood, two black eyes already blooming, and his T-shirt was ripped almost completely down the middle.

"Why did he leave?" he asked, pinching his nose and leaning forward to stop the bleeding.

"He chose greed over violence," Abuela said. She eased back down on a nearby pew with a sigh.

Wyn darted over to Abuela's side and reached into her pocket, slowly pulling out a long shard of stained glass. "I found this up by the altar," she explained. "Hopefully we can get this rope off before he comes back."

Abuela held up her arms. The rope was thick and knotted. But Wyn started sawing away, careful not to cut Abuela's hands or her own with the glass.

We crowded around Abuela as Wyn worked, Franklin at our backs, partially forgotten.

And then there was a massive boom.

Chapter 20

The ground trembled, and Wyn screamed and dropped her makeshift knife. I watched through the far window as the old mines beneath us began to collapse under the weight of the construction equipment and the mud, opening up like a sinkhole behind the chapel. We watched in shock as the mines sucked Franklin—still perched on the excavator—deep into the hole, his screams barely audible over the driving rain.

"Oh my god," Abuela whispered.

"When the mines were closed," Max said in a near whisper, "it happened so suddenly that they left everything behind—including the dynamite."

As if on cue, there was a second, even larger explosion, and fire, smoke, and dirt billowed up from the hole where Franklin had just disappeared.

The walls of the chapel shook with the force of the blast. Glass and wood splinters rained down on us as the chapel—which was barely standing as it was—took the brunt of the explosion.

And then I smelled smoke.

"Oh my god."

The far wall of the chapel, the one closest to where Franklin had been digging, had gone up in flames. Fire was climbing the sides of the chapel, eating up every inch of wood and glass and paper it could get its hands on. The construction lamp light bulb blew with a loud pop, and suddenly the fire was the only light in the room.

"We've got to get out of here," Max said. His voice was oddly calm.

"The glass, it broke," Wyn said, sounding infinitely more panicked. She was grappling along on the floor, trying to find the shard she had been using to cut Abuela's ropes.

"We can untie her later. We've got to go!" I shouted. I ran to the doors, forgetting for just a moment that Franklin had chained them. We were trapped, and the black smoke was growing thicker by the second.

Abuela began to cough, and I slammed my shoulder against the thick wooden doors over and over. They didn't budge.

"We're not going to be able to get out that way," Max cried. "We have to go up!"

I ran back toward Max and looked up. He was pointing to a row of windows near the front of the chapel that I hadn't noticed before—a good fifteen feet off the ground.

I swung around looking for another option—any other option. But there was none. The only exit was chained from the outside, and the rear windows we'd been watching Franklin through were consumed in flames. Every other window in the chapel had been boarded up or was too high off the ground to reach.

Wyn moaned. "We're going to die in here. I can't believe we're going to die in here."

"Abbott!" I screamed, grabbing her by the shoulders and looking her straight in the eyes. "We are NOT going to die. But you gotta keep it together, okay?"

She gulped and nodded.

"Now help me move one of these benches."

The three of us half dragged, half pulled a heavy wooden pew across the floor and set it directly beneath the window. The stone of the chapel was keeping the fire from spreading too quickly, but in a space this small, the smoke would kill us long before we burned to death. A cold comfort.

Max climbed onto the pew and held out his hands toward

us. "Ladies first. I'll lift you guys up, and then you can pull me up once you're on the other side."

"Abuela first," I said quickly. She had moved to sit on the stone floor near the door, the farthest she could get from the smoke and flames. But her head was lulling to one side, and she could barely keep her robe held up in front of her face.

"Abuela!" I screamed. But the fire ate up my voice just as quickly as it had the wooden beams. I went to try again, but I started choking on the smoke, which was thicker than it had been just a moment ago. We were running out of time.

I stumbled my way to Abuela and dragged her to her feet. We made our way back to Max, but Wyn had disappeared.

"Wyn?!" I cried.

"Tig, she's okay!" Max grabbed my shoulder. "I boosted her up already. Abuela will need help getting down with her hands still tied."

I nodded quickly and helped Abuela to the pew and then on top of Max's shoulders, thanking whatever saint this chapel belonged to for his growth spurt this summer. Abuela swayed, unable to balance herself, but Max held her thighs firmly and rose to his feet.

I watched, my face buried in my elbow, as Wyn's pale arms appeared on the other side of the high windows and helped ease Abuela from Max's shoulders to the safety of the hotel grounds.

"Okay, Tig, now you," Max said before doubling over, his whole body racked with coughs.

"Nope, you."

"We don't have time for this!" he cried.

As if to prove his point, a wooden beam from the rafters fell to the floor between us with a crash, engulfing the pews beneath it in flames. On the stone walls, the fire had been somewhat contained. But now, with rows upon rows of hearty wooden benches and old hymnals at its disposal, the fire was free.

And I was blocked off from the last remaining exit.

"Tig!" Max screamed.

"Go!" I called back. "Get out and try to open the door from the outside!"

I knew Max well enough to know that he didn't want to leave me. But what choice did he have? A literal wall of fire stood between him and me, and there was no way I was getting through it.

"Meet me at the door!" I finally heard Max shout. And I watched until his feet finally disappeared through the high window.

But in the minute it took me to see Max to safety, my exit

path had started to close. The fire was completely unchecked now, the whole congregation area in flames. If I didn't go now, I might not make it to the door, even if Max and Wyn somehow managed to unchain it.

I pulled my shirt up around my nose and mouth and took as deep a breath as possible in the smoke. And then I made a break for it.

The fire nipped at my hair and clothes as I raced down the aisle, dodging the ashes falling from the remaining ceiling beams. Beams that could fall at any moment.

I could barely see—the smoke nearly a solid wall now—but I could hear the chains rattling on the other side of the door. Or perhaps it was wishful thinking. I was getting lightheaded, and every breath was like a knife in my chest.

With just steps to the door, I tripped and fell to my hands and knees, my bones cracking on the stone floor. I choked out a sob. *At least I saved Abuela,* I thought as spots began to swim in front of my eyes.

Then I felt a rush of air on my face as the doors swung open.

I looked up and saw two figures in the doorway, shrouded by the smoke rushing out into the night sky. I began to crawl forward. I could make it. We might actually all make it home tonight.

And then another beam fell.

Chapter 21

I fell backward, on my elbows this time. I turned to shield my face from the flames licking now just inches from me. And that's when I spotted it, the thing I had tripped over: Franklin's messenger bag, somehow untouched, sticking out from beneath one of the sole surviving pews.

The sight of it was somehow the jolt I needed. This dumb treasure had nearly killed everyone that I loved tonight. I sure as hell wasn't going to let it kill me, too.

I flung the bag's strap across my body and rose to my feet. And then, without thinking, I raced toward the beam, channeling every moment of Olympic hurdling my dad had ever made me watch.

I sailed over the beam, just barely, and flew into Wyn's and Max's arms in the doorway. They pulled me from the chapel, practically dragging me out into the rain and across the hill.

I turned to see the chapel fully engulfed behind us and Abuela nowhere in sight.

"Abuela—" but I was cut off by a coughing fit.

"She's okay, she's okay," Wyn reassured me. She rubbed my back, getting me through the worst of the coughing.

"Abuela is over at the hotel," Max said. "She's waiting for you."

I ran the rest of the distance, my smoke-filled lungs be damned.

When I spotted her, sitting behind a sheet of heavy plastic out of the rain, I raced into her arms (now miraculously untied) and gave her the hug I've been needing for days.

Abuela heaved out a long sigh when I finally went to extract myself from her arms. Her next breath was shaky and wet. Max, Wyn, and I kept the stillness of a church as she wept.

"So much pain and death," she said to herself, and shook her head. "The price of this treasure has been too great."

"We need to go," I said gently. "There's no way people didn't hear those explosions. We've gotta get out of here before we have too many questions to answer. And if we want to find the treasure, we have to do it tonight."

I lifted up the bag slung across my body, and Wyn and Max, noticing it for the first time, gasped.

Abuela shook her head and wiped her eyes, then suddenly looked at me in concern as if really seeing me for the first time. "That man deserved what happened to him." She reached out and touched the ring of bruises around my neck. They had probably darkened significantly since Franklin had been in our house. I had nearly forgotten about my previous encounter with Franklin after the events of the last few hours, but if Abuela could still see the marks through the smoke and dirt covering my body, I assumed they didn't look great.

"It's okay," I said, covering her trembling hand with my own. "He's gone. You don't have to worry about me."

Abuela shook her head. "I will *always* worry about you, Tig. It's my job," she said simply.

Abuela took a deep breath and heaved herself up. She stretched her arms up high, then swung them around to loosen the joints, wincing as her stiff muscles pulled at the motion.

"Okay," she said resolutely. "We have to get going, but first, we'll need supplies. This is a construction zone, so they should have what we need. We need a small shovel, screwdrivers—Phillips and flathead—protective gloves, a knife or some other kind of prying tool, maybe a hammer if you can find one."

Abuela continued rattling off items, and Wyn and I scattered, grabbing everything we could find in the dim light of the construction site.

"What do we need all this for?" I asked.

"We never knew what we'd have to do or where a clue or treasure would be, so Noel and I always planned for every scenario," she said firmly. "You don't want to be caught without the proper tool—we learned that lesson the hard way in '68."

Wyn and I raised our eyebrows at each other, but I decided not to ask.

"I know this isn't really the most pressing issue," Max said. "But if someone finds a spare shirt lying around, can you send it my way? This is not the most fashionable look." He pulled the two smoky and blood-spattered halves of his shirt out demonstratively. They were hanging around his unscathed neckline like some kind of weird collar.

"You're telling me you'd be willing to wear some smelly old construction worker's T-shirt?" Wyn asked doubtfully.

"I don't know. I feel like it would be pretty iconic if we found the treasure while I was cosplaying as a member of the Village People," he replied, grinning.

"You need *more* coverage, not less," Abuela insisted forcefully. She took off her bathrobe and handed it to Max. "Put it on backward. We do not have all night."

We packed every conceivable thing we might need, from face masks and portable fans to gloves and a power drill. Max tied Abuela's belt around her backward robe and stood with his arms akimbo. He looked delighted. Wyn had found a large hammer to defend herself, which she was practicing swinging in the corner. Abuela leaned down and picked up a crowbar.

"Torreses have good arms," Abuela said with a nod. "Use a firm grip, especially if you're wearing gloves."

I hefted the crowbar in my hand, and it felt like destiny.

"So where are we going?"

"Hold your horses, mija. Let's get out of this rain," Abuela said, leading us into a partially finished section of the Montague Hotel. The plastic was still flapping in the wind against the far wall, but there was a small alcove where moonlight could shine in and it was dry. Rain was pounding forcefully on the roof, and I heard the first sirens wailing far in the distance, the smell of smoke still strong in the air.

"Give me my necklace," Abuela demanded. I lifted the delicate chain from around my neck—thank god I hadn't lost it in the fire—and handed it over. But Abuela was busy digging out the map and spyglass from the bag I had rescued from the chapel.

Wyn and Max crowded around her as she spread the map out on the partially finished wood floor, wiping away streaks of sawdust. Then she twisted off the bottom of the spyglass, put her chain against the bottom, and pressed it in hard. Abuela knocked the spyglass against the floor a couple of times to really wedge it inside and then twisted the bottom back on.

"I can't believe no one knew you had the lens all these years," I said reverently. "Mr. Green thought it had been lost to time."

"That's what I wanted them to think, now wasn't it?" Abuela grinned, and it made her face look decades younger.

"It works better when you're looking at the map by candlelight, but one of your phones will have to do," Abuela said.

Wyn pulled up her flashlight app and shined it on the map. Then Abuela leaned down to put her eye to the spyglass and squinted. A smile spread across her face as she saw exactly what she was looking for.

"Here." She handed the spyglass to me.

I crouched down closer to the map, took a deep breath, and put the spyglass to my eyes. I was surprised to find that with Abuela's pendant inserted, the glass was dark, almost like sunglasses. There was writing on the map, but it was incredibly faint. There were two strings of words leading across town, from one riddle location to the next. The first string was in dark brown that was visible without the spyglass, and the second was lighter than the map itself, like it had been sun-bleached onto the paper. The words ran parallel to each other until the final destination; then they split off in two directions. The dark letters led directly to the chapel, where Franklin Baker had met his doom. The light-colored text swerved off and doubled back toward town and ended at . . . the courthouse. In a tight cramped hand below it, someone had written "earth."

I handed the spyglass to Wyn so she could take a look.

"We were right . . ." I said, in wonder. "*A Vindication of the Rights of Women.* But it's on a different level than the clues said."

Abuela looked at me in surprise. "You solved the final riddle?"

I shrugged, and Abuela took a moment to squeeze me tight. "My smart, beautiful girl." She rose wearily from her knees and looked around at us in turn. "Now let's go find a treasure."

Chapter 22

The rain had slowed to a soft drizzle by the time we left the Montague Hotel, the sirens growing louder in the distance. We opted to walk rather than be caught driving away from a crime scene in a dead woman's car. We'd have to talk to the police eventually, but we still had work to do first.

Walking through patches of streetlights beneath the shadows of the trees felt clandestine, even though we'd done it many nights before. The air felt different, charged with anticipation and apprehension in equal measures. It didn't feel right to talk—to interrupt the silence with chatter that was less important than our mission. In this stillness, my entire body ached—the bumps and bruises left by the violence of Mr. Baker's hands, the burning in my calves from the unexpected run, and hunger pangs from not having stopped to eat.

Adrenaline had fueled me for hours, and it was trickling down to the last drop. But I still felt very awake, my heart was still beating fast, and I could tell I wasn't alone in that.

The town seemed strange suddenly, on this side of the bridge of information. The cozy houses and well-maintained sidewalks weren't a backdrop to me anymore. Every residence we passed seemed to burn with secrets, the small-town charm melting away like seeing the edge of a set. Their existence a palimpsest over the real world I now knew existed beyond them. I wondered, for the first time, how many people knew about The Hunt and its bloody history and had just stayed quiet—ignoring the stories as they went to church and mowed their lawns.

I looked at Abuela's silhouette as she walked in front of us. She was still in the nightgown she'd been wearing when she was kidnapped, but she'd managed to scrape her hair into a tight bun and throw on a pair of old leather boots we'd found in the trunk of Noel's car, oiled and maintained with care as if she knew they would one day be used again.

I could practically see Noel marching in gray beside her, rope and pistol at the ready, a ghost to the cause of adventure and vengeance. Haunting the steps of her dearest love, who would never be truly alone.

The courthouse loomed ahead of us, old and white, with

large pillars and crumbling stone stairs. The windows were dark and promising.

"The courthouse closed at six," Max said, his voice unnaturally loud in the charged silence. "Are we breaking in?" I looked around the block, but the street was mostly empty. It was a part of town that was busiest during the workday and almost completely abandoned at night by the residents who worked there.

Abuela hummed. "The founder's treasure was intended to be found by a 'clever everyman,' so they aren't located in places you need wealth or power to access. And now that we know the treasure's real location, we can focus our search on the first floor of the courthouse, either inside the building or outside it. That's where all the 'earth' clues are located."

Instead of approaching the front door, Abuela led us around the back of the building and to a small box.

"Phillips screwdriver," she demanded.

Wyn pulled it from the bag slung over her shoulder and smacked it into Abuela's palm, like the competent scrub nurse in a hospital drama.

Abuela knelt down with a whoosh of breath and unscrewed the face of the box. Then she jammed the screwdriver underneath, and a metal wire snapped with a twang. She pulled the face down gingerly with her gloved hands, turned a knob, and flipped a switch.

"Tape."

I dug out a roll of duct tape and handed it to her. Abuela taped the face of the box back on.

"Cut the power, and the alarm system is shut down with the rest of the building. If you cut the wire of the alarm, it still notifies the authorities," Abuela explained. She paused, then looked up at Wyn. "Do not teach me to regret doing this in front of you."

"Yes, ma'am," Wyn said, looking at me and Max in confusion about why she was being singled out for reprimand. Max shrugged.

"You take the outside of the building, and I'll look inside. If you find anything, come get me," Abuela said.

"There's more space to cover inside. What if we just split up? You and me inside and Max and Wyn outside?"

"There is more *risk* inside," Abuela said firmly. "We have a half hour before the power needs to be turned back on."

She put her hands on my shoulders and squeezed. "You don't need me to be at your side. You can do this." Then she lumbered to her feet with a small groan of pain and hobbled toward the entrance.

"Where do we even start?" Max said as Abuela disappeared inside.

I dug the small shovel we'd found at the construction site out of my bag. "Well, if it's supposed to be on ground level somewhere, I'm thinking whatever we need to find is in the foundation or buried under one of the floor tiles inside. It may have shifted a bit since the building is, like, two hundred years old, but it shouldn't be that much of a downslide. They would have rebuilt this building like the rest of them if the foundation had moved more than a couple feet."

I hit the shovel against the lowest stonework underneath the circuit. It gave a solid scraping sound. "Yeah, let's just hit all around the outside of the building and if anything sounds hollow, we try to dig it out. Don't be too loud, though."

The courthouse was closely surrounded by dense decorative foliage that shielded us all mostly from view, but a bunch of loud banging would be suspicious regardless if people could see us or not.

Max, Wyn, and I split up—Max checking the rocks with the end of the wrench, Wyn gently hitting them with her hammer, and me continuing with Abuela's shovel. It wasn't quiet work at all. But I could tell we were all trying our best. A piece of the facade chipped off after a really enthusiastic whack, but there was nothing underneath it.

Then my phone vibrated in my pocket.

It was a text from Abuela. It only said one word: *Inside.*

Chapter 23

I sprinted around the building, collecting Max and Wyn, and we ducked inside, closing the door tight behind us.

Abuela sat in the center of the lobby, cross-legged with a commandeered air-filtration mask on. In one hand she had what appeared to be a box cutter, and in the other was a small handheld drill. Tossed to the side was a crowbar. One of the courthouse's granite tiles had been placed gingerly to the side, leaving a large square hole in the floor.

"Masks," she said, and Wyn, Max, and I quickly put on our masks as well. As we got closer, dust from the tile grout swirled up into the air with every step.

Abuela tapped at the side of the hole.

"You solved the riddle—you do the honors," she said.

I glanced at Max and Wyn. "We did it together," I said.

Abuela's eyes crinkled with mirth. "Good thing the box doesn't look light."

Max, Wyn, and I crouched around the hole and pulled a large trunk out of the floor. It was extremely heavy. Max had a whole side to himself, but Wyn and I had to work together to lift the other. We dropped it hard, and it crashed to the floor with a loud boom.

Abuela looked at her watch. "Ten minutes," she hissed.

The box was fully metal, corroded on all sides, and had no visible latch.

"How do we open it?" Wyn whispered.

"I don't know. Try hitting it with your hammer," I suggested.

"That's going to be way too loud," Max complained. "I'm just going to try tugging it."

He crouched down and slapped both hands on either side of the lid and pulled, straining. Wyn hit the side of it that Max's body wasn't blocking with the hammer, and there was an audible crack.

"It's clay! They sealed it with clay!" I exclaimed.

Wyn continued to bang around the sides of the box while Max maintained the tension. I stuck the shovel into the gaps and pried the lid up all the way around the perimeter of the box until there was an ominous squeak, and an earthen scent filled the room. Unprepared for the release of tension, Max fell backward as the lid broke free, and the room was filled with a puff of powder.

"Ugh!" Wyn coughed in disgust. "Human dust!"

Abuela peered into the box and lifted off a thin layer of fabric, which almost immediately disintegrated in her hands. She clutched the rotting threads to her chest and closed her eyes.

"I wish Noel was here," she said quietly.

The founder's treasure was spread out before us, dusty and free. His bones were neatly piled, arms and legs tied with an organic-looking cord, his skull placed in the cradle of his own arms. It was missing two back teeth, and he had an almost comically large forehead. Along with his bones, there were three homespun bags, each extremely heavy; a book with a long ribbon trailing from the pages; and a photograph, almost completely washed out with age.

I picked up the picture and shined my light on it. It was of an older man and middle-aged woman, holding each other around the waist and beaming. He was shorter than her and stout, with a giant forehead ringed with wild tufts of white hair. She was tall and kind-looking with deep smile lines on her face. They were clearly terribly in love: the founder and his wife.

"Holy shit!" Wyn said.

I looked up. Wyn was holding a nugget of silver the size of an eggplant in one hand, the flashlight from her phone shooting sparkles of light off its massive surface. She placed the silver in her lap and quickly opened the next bag, which had a similarly sized nugget of gold. Wyn reached into the last bag and pulled out a strange lumpy metal.

"Put that down!" Abuela shouted in alarm. "Go wash your hands. Quickly. Quickly!" Wyn dropped the metal and ran off into the courthouse to find the bathroom. Abuela scooped the metal back into the bag with her gloved hands, removed her gloves, and put on a fresh pair.

"That's raw lead," she said, sighing in relief. "It's harder to absorb through your skin, but no one should take any chances. They weren't as knowledgeable about the effects of lead as we are today. Wyn will be fine, but do not touch this bag, and we aren't taking it home."

"Yikes," Max said, looking down the hall where Wyn had disappeared.

I handed the photograph of the founder and his wife to Abuela. "Look at them; they were so cute."

She took the photograph and gazed at it with soft eyes. I dug back into the box and picked up the book inside. I flipped through it quickly. It looked like it was a journal, mostly full of recipes. I opened the page that the ribbon was on. Next to a—quite frankly horrendous—recipe for a licorice cake was another recipe:

<u>Craftmaker's Pie</u>

You will need:
1 ream of paper
2 c. of card stock
3½ tsp of string
1 tbsp of paste
1 sharp knife
2 paper fillings

Cut one piece of card stock to a frame roughly the size of your book. Cover the frame with paste and adhere to adequately cut card stock. Insert your filling, not too sweet or too thick, folded tight. Adhere to cover card stock and paste liberally over with decorative paper. Poke forty holes in your ream and sew deftly to bind. Paste to spine. Age and serve well done.

Love,
Minnie

It was written in a format to match the rest of the book, such that if the reader was careless, he wouldn't have bothered to look closer. I picked up Abuela's box cutter and flipped the book to the back cover, which was slightly thicker than the front cover.

"What are you doing?" Max cried. "Don't ruin it!"

"There's something in here," I said, cutting the cover deftly around the edge. I lifted the decorative paper up, and just as I suspected, there was a tightly folded paper inside it. I unfolded the thin sheet to four times its size, and a letter fell out.

I started reading aloud as Wyn made her way back to the lobby.

Wanderer,

Time is a gift both taken and given when half of a pair expires. For the beloved: the time spent at the foot of the fire among family and confidants, the pleasure of days, the sweetness of aging. For a widow: nights in cold, home in silence, hours for retribution. I know not what madness holds these cursed lands, what makes men into beasts which sup on blood and greed, jackals, and carrion eaters in our midst. But good men should not have to live as though their houses were wilderness.

On the day we claimed these lands, my husband said that the sun felt warm on our skin and the soil was soft enough for our bairn's soles. The houses we built were good and strong. It was a kind time.

But there must be something in the water that does not make its presence known until time has passed, or perhaps the Lord was not pleased with the purity of our souls. But one by one, hatefulness grew from the soft soil of our townspeople's hearts, and the sun wasn't bright enough to purge nighttime's sin from the day. These curs, twice damned, brutish as coarse cloth, learned of the riches we let lay in the mines and grew fierce with it.

Not caring that the miners dropped dead when approaching it as though the entrance were enchanted, it tore at them and they pursued my beloved like demons until the joy faded from his eyes. He rode hard to the state capital to secure our land rights, despite his advanced age and frangible temperament. Barely had he made it back, certificate clutched in hand, that they beset upon him. Uncaring of his dependents or God's law.

A day has not gone by that I have not hated them.

The miners feared death at the hand of whoever would take hold of the mine in my beloved's stead, and this granted me their allegiance—though I am woman, and not in possession of power nor title. We destroyed the mine and blocked the exits; scarce had three days passed that his body went cold.

With barely time remaining, from small hours to daybreak, we planted the seeds of his memory. In the form of his favorite books, and at the very last, one of mine. For had I been granted the rights to hold property in my own hands, there would have been no need to fear for a cruel death in the dark heart of the earth serving the greed of Man. My husband's killers, who had no such love in their hearts for books or justice or the beauty of the world, would never be able to get what they wanted most—that which you hold in your hand. A prize hard won and waiting. Our beloved town and all that lies beneath it.

With love, from Minnie and her Henry

I turned over the letter, but it was blank. The large paper behind it was baroquely decorated like a bond.

"What is it?" Wyn asked.

"It's . . . I think it's the full land rights for the town . . ." I said, squinting close at the tiny flourishing print. "The founder's treasure *is* the town . . . and the millions of dollars of silver beneath it."

Abuela brushed her fingertips across the photograph of the couple. "Silver that no one can touch unless they decide to destroy the town first."

Max startled, dropping the enormous silver nugget onto the ground.

"Is the mine haunted?" Wyn asked, scrunching her nose up in disbelief.

Abuela shook her head. "Silver isn't like diamonds or emeralds. It doesn't just come in veins alone. It's often mixed with other ores like gold, lead, sulfur, and also mercury. The miners were inhaling mercury gas. If whoever found the treasure decided to mine for the rest of the silver, they would put the lives of every man, woman, and child on its soil at risk.

"Minnie's treasure was a love letter but also a clever test of greed to protect the legacy of a kind man. Whoever she might have been, she was a giant among us all."

"What do we do now?" I asked, folding the paper back up and placing it inside the book.

Abuela looked up at the ceiling in thought.

"Alan and Noel deserve a part in this. I wish I could give it to them," she murmured.

Wyn reached over and squeezed Abuela's shoulder tenderly.

"How much energy do you have left tonight?" I asked Wyn and Max.

"Not a lot, to be honest," Max replied with a dry laugh.

"Enough to put this whole thing to rest," Wyn said resolutely.

I pulled on my gloves and reached for the contaminated bag of lead; then I took the land rights and Minnie's letter out of the recipe book and shoved them into the bag, pulling the drawstring tight.

"We'll bury this above Mr. Wyatt's coffin," I announced. "Even with the rain, the fresh dirt should be easy to dig through. Not only will it be way more difficult for anyone else to find, but the elements will probably destroy the paper relatively quickly, leaving just the lead for the greedy . . . But at least Mr. Wyatt will be united with the treasure to the very end. And he got his dying wish—The Hunt is over."

I gingerly wrapped the lead bag in a piece of plastic sheeting from the construction site and slid it into my bag.

"We can bring the box of bones to the mayor," I continued. "Give him the recipe book and tell him that the founder's treasure has been found. Then we can go out of town and trade in the gold and silver nuggets for cash—even, four-way split. That sound fair?"

"Yep," Wyn said, clambering to her feet. She stretched her arms and cracked her shoulder.

"Cool. Okay. Grave digging. First bone dust, now grave digging," Max griped, turning to Abuela. "Can't I just stay here with you and help put the tile back?"

Abuela closed her eyes again and sighed, smiling.

"I'll be right behind you. I just want to savor this victory on my own for a moment," Abuela replied. She leaned over and gently nudged Max in the shoulder. "Don't be a spoilsport. Be an adventurer while you're still young enough to enjoy it."

"Yeah, Max, don't be a spoilsport," Wyn said, pushing Max's other shoulder and laughing when he pushed her back.

While Max and Wyn bickered and packed up the rest of the supplies, I took a moment to hug my abuela tight and rock with her back and forth. Something had changed between us, and all at once I felt much older. Like her granddaughter of course, but now, somehow, also like her friend.

The mud covered my arms past my elbows, and my legs past my knees, fingertips smarting from the pressure of pushing flesh into soil. But there we stood: with the red light of dawn at our backs and with a hole to the center of the world.

I took the contaminated parcel out of my bag and tossed it in. It landed onto the wood of Mr. Wyatt's casket with a soft thump. I peeled off my gloves as well, and they fluttered down into the dark.

The silence of this ending was like waking up to a morning of snow.

"I wish I had gotten to know you better," I said.

Max and Wyn said nothing.

We used the last of our strength, shaking and cold from the night air, to push the ground back into place. Mr. Wyatt and Minnie's treasure, at rest, at last.

And here we stand at the end of the road. At the end of a story that started with love and ended with love, and yet I don't feel any different. The darkness still lives in Hollow Falls, just the same as we all do. This town, where questions just lead to more questions and you get answers you sort of wish you hadn't . . .

After we found the treasure in the courthouse, we went straight home with the bones and the recipe book: Minnie's treasure of recipes brought together by the townspeople at the birth of our home.

We took the book to Mayor Highsmith the next day with the body as proof that we located the treasure. It wasn't the big flashy gold and silver treasure that I'm sure everyone was hoping for, but it was valuable and it was ours. He accepted the bones for proper reburial but gave us back the recipe book after tearing out one page: the disgusting licorice-flavored Anise Founder's Day Cake. I tried to stop him, but you'll have to deal with that in our bakeries next month. I, for one, will be skipping that particular dessert this Founder's Day, town tradition be damned.

Another thing we might have to deal with is tourists. As you may know, after the whole thing with Franklin and his Hunt-inspired murder spree came to light, our local author-in-residence, Judah Beckett, used the publicity to his advantage and sold his book for a hefty advance. I've already seen a couple visitors prowling around town, looking at sites of some of Hollow Falls's most gruesome crimes, like our trauma exists just for their amusement. I'd like to think it'll die down, but I have a feeling there may be more to come . . .

Judah is refusing to tell national media (and rumor has it, even his own editor) whether the events detailed in his book are real, but true-crime aficionados don't care. They've been wandering our streets in search of the macabre, like Hollow Falls is their own personal amusement park. Who knows if they'll find it . . . But they should hope that they don't.

Sometimes I wonder . . . is this even

something I should be doing? Sticking my nose where it doesn't belong? Tracking down people who will kill me without a second thought? This podcast means a lot to me, and I've done some good, sure. But so many people have gotten hurt along the way. It would be easier and less painful to just let the police handle it, or watch how events unfurl from afar . . .

But what happens when things fall through the cracks—when *people* fall through the cracks? Someone has to stand up and take on the risk, to seek justice when everyone around them has gotten tired of fighting. Of course, there are things I wish I hadn't seen or experienced—and things I wish the people I loved didn't have to see or experience, either—but being close to death like I have, it changes you as a person.

I know I haven't lived here long, but the people of Hollow Falls are a community. *We* are a community. And if my aunt Beth taught me anything, it's that the people in communities need to take care of one another. If this podcast is how I can do my part to find justice for people who need it, if it can help stop monsters who hurt people for their own gain, then so be it. I don't care about the cost because this kind of feels like my destiny, as cheesy as that sounds. To deny my purpose and to leave all this buried in my past wouldn't do anyone any good. Especially with so much danger yet to be discovered here.

Last season's Lit Killer case had danger lurking in the dark corners of our town—a true-crime lover's paradise. And with everything that I've seen since then and what I've read in Judah's book, I have to wonder: Is there anywhere truly safe in Hollow Falls? Or will we be doomed to pay the price of the sins of our forefathers forever?

I don't know, but one day I promise I'll find out . . .

I'm Tig Torres, and this is *Lethal Lit*.

Epilogue

"I can't believe we finished in time," Max whined. "Doing two all-nighters in less than a week has probably shaved at least four years off my life span. I can actually feel my cells dying."

Wyn let out a wordless groan in agreement.

"Those stupid kids better read this entire edition of the *Talon* or I'm going to start swinging in the hallway," she replied, sliding down the side of my bed to land in a heap on the floor. Max reached over and caught her laptop before it slid down with her.

"God, be careful, Wyn. Anyway, I can't believe Ella turned in her articles early," Max said. "She's so infuriating."

I laughed. "Yeah, yeah. But while I hate to admit it, we couldn't have done this without her. She saw how wiped we were after the founder's treasure stuff and formatted the entire paper so that all we had to do was slot our pieces in. You gotta admit, it was a hell of a lifesaver."

While it was still taking some getting used to, I did find myself less surprised and less annoyed every time Ella showed up somewhere with Wyn or whenever we crossed paths at the diner or at the *Talon*. I guess capturing not one but two serial killers together really does bring people closer. Who knew?

The two weeks before school had thundered past so quickly after the founder's treasure case that I had forgotten we still had to draft the first edition of the school paper until Max called in hysterics. With only forty-eight hours until printing, we'd been scrambling to get the paper thrown together like the dogs of hell were at our heels.

Luckily, we had lots of content for the front page.

Max yawned loudly. "How much longer until we can move to the slumber part of this slumber party?" he complained.

"Ooo, can you ask Abuela if we can order a pizza?" Wyn asked with a glimmer in her eyes.

"I could eat," I said, rubbing my eyes and getting up to stretch.

"Cheese and pepperoni on mine, please," Max said.

"Ugh, you guys can share that. I want a veggie lovers," Wyn griped.

"Okay, two veggie pizzas and one cheese and pepperoni coming up," I said tiredly, and stumbled to the door.

"It doesn't matter what you told them, Sofia. You made a vow."

I stopped opening the door and pushed it most of the way closed before peeking my head out to see who was in the hallway. In front of Abuela's room, fully dressed in a crisp suit even though it was in the middle of the night on a Sunday, was Mr. Green. I hadn't even heard him come into the house.

"But the children will be disappointed. I'm supposed to be heading into the city tomorrow to trade this in," Abuela whispered.

"The book and payment, Sofia. I won't ask again," Mr. Green said in a stern voice I hadn't heard him use before. I closed the door even more and watched as Abuela handed Mr. Green the gold nugget we'd found in the courthouse and the founder's wife's recipe book.

"Does she know about Ana?" Mr. Green asked.

"No, Charlie. I wouldn't . . . you know I wouldn't," Abuela said, shaking her head. "It was bad enough she almost found out about Irena. I'll keep a closer eye on her, I promise."

"What's going on?" Wyn said loudly behind me. I startled and pushed the door closed, but before it touched the doorframe, the door stopped.

Mr. Green was suddenly standing in the doorway, holding the door open the last centimeter with an iron grip. He moved so much faster and so much quieter than I ever thought possible. Almost faster than Franklin. I stared at him through the crack, frozen, silent. Mr. Green smiled kindly, his eyes crinkling, then put a single finger up to his lips.

"Have a good night, Sofia," he called loudly down the hall.

Then he pulled the door all the way closed, jerking it powerfully out of my grasp with his incredible strength. When I managed to yank it back open, the hall was empty.

I looked down the hall in the other direction, and Abuela was standing in her doorway, looking back at me.

I cleared my throat. "Wyn and Max are hungry—can we get pizza?" I asked.

She visibly relaxed. "Oh! Of course, give me a moment to go get my wallet."

Abuela disappeared into her room to hunt for her purse. I turned back to Wyn and Max, who were sitting up in the bed curiously.

"We have another case," I said seriously.

"What?"

"Let's order for pickup. I'll tell you while we're walking over." I grabbed my sweatshirt and put it on.

"Can't we have even a single night off?" Wyn huffed, covering her face with my pillow.

"Maybe this time, we'll catch the killer *before* someone gets killed," said Max hopefully.

I thought about the tone of Mr. Green's voice and the trembling in Abuela's.

"I wouldn't bet on it if I were you," I said, tucking my recorder into my pocket. "In Hollow Falls, you would always lose."

Acknowledgments

Thank you so much to my wonderful agent, Eric, who keeps me on the level. My supportive partner, Kyle, who I wouldn't be able to write without. The entire Scholastic and *Lethal Lit* team for their insight, persistence, and their deep love of Tig and her wonderful family of friends. Lastly, I would like to thank Samantha Swank for holding my umbrella during every brain storm. Your input was invaluable and your contributions to this novel were vital.

About the Author

Photo credit: Jasemine Denise Photography

K. Ancrum is the author of the award-winning thriller *The Wicker King*; a lesbian romance, *The Weight of the Stars*; and the Peter Pan thriller *Darling*. K. is a Chicago native passionate about diversity and representation in young adult fiction. She currently writes most of her work in the lush gardens of the Art Institute of Chicago.

THAT'S NOT THE END OF THE MYSTERY!
Top Shows
See All
EEP
Lethal Lit
A TIG TORRES MYSTERY
Lethal Lit
Einhorn's Epic Productions
DAUGHTERS of DC
DUPONT PREP
EEP
Daughters of DC
Einhorn's Epic Productions
SEE YOU IN YOUR NIGHTMARES
EEP
See You In Your Nightmares
Einhorn's Epic Productions
Follow Tig's adventures in the Lethal Lit podcast, and jump into these great audio thrillers next!
LISTEN NOW FOR
FREE!
ANYWHERE YOU GET YOUR PODCASTS
EINHORN'S EPIC PRODUCTIONS
iHeart RADIO
Brought to you by Einhorn's Epic Productions & iHeartRadio
Follow Einhorn's Epic Productions at @eintropolis
© 2022 Einhorn's Epic Cookies, LLC and other rightsholders as applicable. All Rights Reserved.